THE FOREST OF DRAKES

SUMMONED TO ANOTHER WORLD AND FORCED TO FIGHT THE DEMON KING

BOOK SIX

JAMES E. WISHER

SAND HILL PUBLISHING

Edited by: Janie Linn Dullard

Cover art by: B-Ro

CHAPTER 1

Danny had given up on keeping track of how long he'd been traveling days ago. Since parting company with the beastfolk, his world had blurred into endless dirt roads, trees, and rolling plains as he ran at a magically enhanced pace that put a galloping horse to shame. In fact, he had become so good at maintaining his physical enhancements that he could run from sunrise to sunset with only a half-hour break for lunch and feel no ill effects the next day.

It was an efficient way to travel, but he'd gotten some weird looks from the merchants and other travelers he left in the dust. Not that he blamed them. After all, how often did you see a crazy person running down the road as if he had the Reaper himself on his tail?

Danny also avoided most of the little towns he passed, though he did stop at a few of the larger ones for a night, both to sleep in a real bed and to gather intel on his destination. To say the Forest of Drakes had a bad reputation would be an understatement. Much like Elfhome, most people considered it a death trap, especially if you ventured too deep. Apparently, the forest served as the drakes' breeding ground and many different species called it home.

Despite the danger, a couple of centuries ago an enterprising group of adventurers built a city called Scale a safe distance from the forest. The Adventurers' Guild there specialized in gathering drake parts for use in various magical projects. Danny hoped to get more detailed information about the forest when he arrived. And he should probably take a job or two just to keep up appearances. He hadn't accepted a proper guild-sponsored mission since leaving the Five Kingdoms. He did hunt and kill an Alpha Wolf, but that didn't count as a mission.

At least the spring weather had remained pleasant. Aside from the occasional passing shower, he'd enjoyed plenty of sun and mild temperatures. The weather, combined with a welcome lack of bandits and monsters, made this the nicest stretch of travel he'd enjoyed since arriving on Valindor.

He didn't trust his good fortune to last.

The thought had barely formed when he sensed six humans directly ahead, standing in the middle of the road. Danny skidded to a stop, sending a cloud of dust flying. The flat land made it easy to see them. They didn't look like bandits—not grubby enough. All six wore pristine heavy plate armor covered in white tabards.

Danny squinted and enhanced his vision further. Uh-oh. Was that Adonael's halo symbol on their chests?

Well, the Reaper had warned him that Heaven wouldn't look kindly on his recent decisions, and he'd already earned a prime spot on Adonael's shit list. Finding a group of knights waiting for him in the middle of the road didn't come as a huge shock.

No sense delaying the inevitable. He pulled the ether-sword out of storage and started walking. When only fifty yards separated them, the central knight stepped forward to meet him.

Did they plan to fight a series of one-on-one matches? That seemed unlikely, but if they wanted to go that route, he wouldn't complain. Danny doubted he'd lose to any man one-on-one.

The lone knight stopped in the middle of the road, his helmet under one arm. Danny ambled up until only a couple of feet separated them. The guy looked about forty, with weathered, leathery skin from spending a lot of time outdoors. Streaks of gray ran through his dark, neatly trimmed beard, making Danny a little self-conscious about the rough, scraggly beard he'd grown during his travels.

"You would be Daniel the Hero," the knight said. "Our Lady Adonael told us we'd find you here."

"That's me," Danny said. "Something I can help you boys with?"

"My name is Sir Hugh Wotton, commander of the Halo Knights in Scale City. Our lady told us you were a man of honor. If you promise to hunt down and slay the demon king and give up on your pointless quest to destroy the summoning circle, we will let you pass."

Danny shook his head. "Sorry, not happening. I told Adonael to her face it wasn't happening, and now I'm telling you. No one else from my world will die for yours, not if I can help it."

"Then it seems battle is unavoidable," Hugh said.

"On the contrary, if you and your men stay out of my way, battle is entirely avoidable. I have no interest in you or any other member of your faith. Swear you'll leave me alone and no one has to die."

"Our orders do not allow it. I would fight you in a duel, but I know enough about your abilities to understand that would lead to my death, and worse, failing this mission." Hugh blew out a breath and shook his head. "Six against one is hardly honorable."

"You seem like a good man," Danny said. "Would you do me a favor?"

"If it's within my power."

"When you see Adonael, would you tell her to stop sending me good men to kill? There are plenty of evil people and monsters for me to fight already."

Hugh snorted. "Bit full of yourself, aren't you, boy? My comrades and I are the finest warriors in Adonael's temple."

"If the six of you sufficed to kill the demon king, I wouldn't have been summoned," Danny said. "I won that fight and I'll win this one, though it will give me a good deal less pleasure."

"I think our discussion is concluded." Hugh turned on his heel and marched back to his fellow knights, back rigidly straight. Looked like Danny offended him.

He sighed. A smart man would run Hugh through from behind before he had a chance to prepare, but Danny couldn't do it. Hugh called him an honorable man and Danny liked to think that was true, at least to an extent. If he truly believed these knights had a hope of beating him, he might've made a different decision.

When Hugh reached his men, they all took a knee and bowed their heads. The prayer didn't last long. When they stood, each knight made the halo symbol above his head and drew his sword. Ether flowed through them as they strengthened their bodies.

Danny lit the ethersword and charged his body with ether until it felt like he might vibrate to pieces.

The ground cracked when he pushed off, charging the knights at full speed.

They split, with two holding their ground, two going left and two right.

The central pair braced themselves to meet his charge.

Danny's blows came fast and precise. First, he knocked their swords out of alignment, then he slashed back at the gap between their helmets and gorgets. Their heads hit the ground a moment later.

The survivors charged in from both directions.

Danny leapt back, hit the ground, and charged them.

All four were quick. They fought well, covering each other's openings. Their swords even resisted the ethersword's blade.

None of it mattered.

A burst of raw ether exploded from Danny, hurling the knights away.

He sprinted after them, little more than a blur.

A vertical slash severed a leg from one man, and a thrust pierced a second's mouth.

Two left, including Hugh.

He had to give the pair credit. Despite witnessing their fellow knights fall, they asked for no mercy. Perhaps they had faith in the reception they'd receive in Heaven.

He gave them no time to gather themselves. One more charge and a pair of slashes ended the fight. Once more, he found himself alone on the road, now surrounded by the dead.

Danny released his magic and sighed. What had Adonael been thinking, sending warriors that weak to fight him? If she wanted him dead surely she could find some method to try that wouldn't result in the deaths of good men.

Well, whatever. He put the ethersword away and got busy cleaning up his mess. It didn't take long to check them for valuables. Their purses held only a few silver coins, but he took it all regardless. On the road, every silver counted. Finally, he loaded their bodies into storage. He'd drop them off at a temple for proper burial. The honorable knights deserved that much at least.

With the road clear once more, Danny set out, this time at an unenhanced walk. He'd used about all the magic he cared to for today.

CHAPTER 2

Around noon the day after his battle with Adonael's knights, Danny spotted dark walls rising in the distance. He assumed he'd reached the city of Scale. As he got closer, the details became clearer. The wall stood about thirty feet tall and half that thick. Towers jutted up even higher every twenty paces or so. A heavy ballista mounted on a swivel stand topped each tower, and guards patrolled the dark stone battlements, bows in hand.

Though much smaller than Discourt, Scale appeared more heavily defended. He suspected being this close to the drakes' breeding ground played a part in their building decisions. With that many ballistae, they should be able to deter all but the strongest drakes.

Danny worked the kinks out of his neck as he approached the city's gate. He still felt a little stiff from yesterday's excessive magic use, but other than that he had no complaints. Thank goodness for a quick recovery. If the temple of Adonael wanted to make more trouble for him, he'd make them regret the decision.

A modest line of wagons and travelers on foot waited outside the gate. Danny stopped a few feet from a heavily armed group of four men. They wore leather armor and sturdy clothes, along with swords, daggers, spears, and a couple of bows.

They had to be adventurers.

One of the men, a grizzled fellow who looked older than Sir Hugh, finally noticed him. Danny offered a polite nod but didn't speak. A chat didn't appeal to him at the moment. Mostly, he wanted to enter the city, find a room, and enjoy a hot meal. After that, he'd locate the Adventurers' Guild and see what he could learn about this part of the world.

Unfortunately for Danny, his taciturn expression did nothing to dissuade the older man from striking up a conversation. "You an adventurer?"

"Yup," Danny said.

"Us too. Where's the rest of your group?"

"I work alone, mostly doing scouting and hunting."

The older man nodded. "Sketchy working alone, especially if you're headed to the forest. Even a young drake can tear a lone man to pieces in a blink. We could use a scout. What say you join up with Evard's Blade?"

The rest of the group had turned to watch the conversation. Danny didn't want to be rude, but he also had no intention of joining a team. "Thanks for the offer, but I'll pass. I've worked in groups before and it seldom ends well. On my own, I have full control over my fate, for better or worse."

One of the younger men bristled. "You saying you're too good for us?"

Danny shifted his gaze to focus on him. "I didn't say that at all. I said I prefer to work alone."

"Steady, Brand," the older man said. "You know the guild's

rules, no fighting with fellow members. If the youngster prefers to work alone, that's his business."

Brand snorted in contempt and spun back around.

"Don't mind him," the older man said. "Brand was just promoted to journeyman and he's got a bit of a chip on his shoulder. Name's Evard and I lead this group."

"Ronin." They shook hands. "I just arrived in the area. From what I've heard, the Forest of Drakes is a deadly place."

"It is that. Still, we just came back from a job over Three Peaks's way and the pay hardly covered the cost of the trip. Dangerous or not, the best money to be made around here is from gathering drake scales. Is that what you're looking to do?"

Danny shrugged. "Hadn't thought much about it. I'm traveling the world and this seemed like an interesting place to visit. I saw a drake once, a big, fire-breathing one. It was crazy."

Evard's eyes bulged. "How the hell did you survive a fire drake?"

"Lucky, I guess. Anyway, I thought it'd be fun to see what some of the others look like. I'm pretty good at stealth magic, so I should be okay. If I can pick up a few scales along the way, I won't say no to easy money."

"You've got guts, kid. I respect that." When their turn came, Evard left Danny alone and went to speak to the guards on duty. They all showed their guild cards and the guards waved them right through.

Danny dug out his card, and as soon as the bored guard saw it, he waved him through as well. He didn't even have to answer any questions. Danny shook his head. Clearly the people in charge of Scale didn't feel the need to worry about either plague bearers or disguised demons sneaking in.

Not that he planned to complain. Danny had had his fill of both over the past few months.

Inside, Scale reminded him more of a large frontier village than a proper city like Discourt. Most of the generally modest buildings had two stories, with businesses on the bottom and living spaces above. Some chickens ran past him. He expected to see a farmer or a kid chasing them, but it looked like they were just wandering around the streets on their own. Weird, but whatever. If they survived until dark, Danny would be impressed.

Putting the odd encounter out of his mind, he went looking for an inn. A place this big had to have a few. Guard patrols, on the other hand, seemed in short supply. Since entering, he hadn't seen anything resembling law enforcement. The people all carried weapons. And not just knives like elsewhere, but swords, axes, and spears as well. The more he saw, the more the city brought to mind an army camp.

He rounded a corner and spotted a big stone building with a sign featuring a crossed sword and wand: the Adventurers' Guild. Well, he hadn't planned to stop by until later, but since he was here, maybe someone knew a good inn.

Danny pushed through the door and entered the common room. Groups of adventurers occupied three tables and the members of Evard's Blade stood at the counter speaking with one of the two clerks. The other clerk, a cute brunette dressed in a pleasantly snug, low-cut green tunic, looked his way. Danny ambled over, his best smile in place, and set his guild card on the counter.

She smiled back. "Welcome to the Scale City Guild. How can I be of service today?"

"I just arrived from Discourt and wanted to get an idea of

what sort of work I can find in the area. I heard about collecting drake scales already, but that's all I know. Also, if you can recommend a good inn, I'd appreciate it."

"I've never heard of Discourt," she said. "Where is it?"

Danny thought for a moment. "Maybe seven hundred miles west of here. I'd say it's about three times the size of Scale, with plenty of rich people, most of whom are completely corrupt. I won't miss much about the place."

"Sounds... interesting."

"It was the prettiest cesspool you've ever seen. I'd rather take my chances with the drakes."

She shivered slightly, drawing Danny's gaze to inappropriate places. "Right, you wanted to know about the area. As you've probably guessed, everything in Scale revolves around the forest, either directly, with adventurers going in to scrounge what they can, or with people supporting them. In some ways, the city itself is an extension of the guild. In fact, our guild master is also the mayor."

"Is that why I had such an easy time getting in?"

"Sure is. The more adventurers there are, the more the guild makes and the better the economy does." She glanced around and lowered her voice. "We also have a pretty high attrition rate, so new people are vital."

Danny could well imagine. "So what sort of jobs are available?"

"You can find them all on the board." She pointed to the ever-present job board on the opposite wall. Papers covered it from top to bottom. "Most are standing bounties on drake parts, but there are also a number of rare plants that grow in the forest. Those are in constant demand. Now and then, a wizard will come in looking for bodyguards, but that's about it."

"And the guild will buy whatever I bring in?" he asked.

"Yup. We also process carcasses if you have the good fortune to find a fresh one. The drakes are constantly fighting over territory and sometimes one of them will die in a match. Someone brings in a partial carcass about once every ten or so years. It always causes quite a fuss."

Danny grinned. "I bet. Well, that all sounds straightforward. I don't suppose you have a map of the forest?"

"We do!" She bent over, giving him a close look at her cleavage. "Here you go."

She set a rolled-up parchment on the counter. Danny spread it out and sure enough, he found a map of the area. Not that it told him much he didn't already know. The forest occupied most of the map and Danny guessed, based on the scale, that it measured over two thousand miles across. That aligned with his estimates from the elf-blood map. Other than Scale, he saw no settlements, though he assumed there had to be farms nearby to support the city.

The sheer size of the forest daunted him. How in the world would he find the ether pool in that?

"The map is two silver coins," she said after he had studied it for a couple of minutes.

"I don't have any local currency. Is there somewhere I can exchange what I have?"

"We can do it here. Let me grab my scale and money box." She hurried away, giving him a glimpse of a pair of legs every bit as nice as what she had up top.

Danny grimaced and looked away. He needed some female companionship and soon.

The clerk returned with a scale, some weights, and a small wooden box. "Here we go. What would you like to trade in?"

Danny always kept one of his large gold coins in his satchel, and he placed it on the counter. "Let's start with this."

Her eyes widened. "I've never seen a gold coin this big. Where did you get it?"

"The Five Kingdoms. That's where I started my career."

"Never heard of that either." She placed the coin on one side of the scale then added weight to the other. When it balanced, she counted out the right amount of smaller gold coins as well as some silvers. "There you go."

"Thanks." Danny slid her two silvers. "For the map."

She added them to the box. "Did you need anything else?"

"Just directions to the nearest inn. I'm starving."

"Sure! The Nest is a couple doors up. A lot of adventurers stay there between jobs, so they're used to a rough clientele." She covered her mouth with her hand. "No offense."

"None taken, Miss..."

"Erin." She extended her hand, and Danny shook it. "I hope you enjoy your visit to Scale, Ronin."

Danny didn't plan on spending that much time in the city, but he nodded. "Thanks."

Parting ways with Erin, Danny walked over to the job board. Two-thirds of the parchments were marked "Do Not Remove." They listed nearly every part of a drake imaginable, along with their respective prices. Scales fetched two gold coins each. Danny tried to remember how big Merrok's scales had been but couldn't quite remember. Half the size of his palm maybe. It also didn't specify payment by species, which seemed odd. Surely every type of drake didn't have the same value.

He scanned the remaining listings. Looked like scales were the cheapest part of the drake. Danny tried to imagine how much a complete carcass would be worth and failed.

As for the standard job requests, one merchant wanted guards for his caravan, while an alchemist needed someone willing to test a new healing potion he'd devised. No way would that second one find any takers in the near future. Danny had learned enough about magic that the thought of drinking an unproven potion made him shudder.

When he finished reading, Danny ducked out of the guild and made the short walk down the street to The Nest. The two-story wooden structure looked well maintained, with freshly painted siding and no gaps in the slate roof. The sign above the door featured a bed with a drake curled around it. Whoever carved it clearly had skill; every detail looked perfect, right down to the individual claws.

Danny pushed the door open and strode into the nearly empty common room. One unfamiliar group sat at a corner table, while Evard's Blade occupied another.

Ignoring both, he headed for the bar, where an attractive middle-aged woman busied herself reorganizing the shelf of alcohol behind it. She smiled as he approached. "Can I get you something, hon?"

"A room for the night and a hot meal would be most welcome, ma'am."

"Then you've come to the right place. A room is three silver coins and includes breakfast. We've got pork and roasted potatoes for a silver coin, and that comes with a small ale."

"That all sounds perfect." Danny handed her the appropriate coins from his new collection and sat on a stool while she went to fetch his food. The cook must've prepared everything in advance, as she returned in less than a minute and set the plate and drink in front of him. "Thanks. Could you tell me where the temple of Adonael is from here?"

"Sure. All the temples are in the city center surrounding the government building. They're clearly marked, so you shouldn't have any trouble finding it."

Danny nodded in thanks and tucked in. He planned to savor his meal and relax, as he seriously doubted that visiting the temple would be enjoyable, especially after he returned their dead knights.

CHAPTER 3

Danny took a deep breath of fresh morning air and turned toward Scale's city center. After a decent night's sleep and a breakfast of bread and bacon, he felt ready to face the day. He wasn't eager by any means, but he was ready. Today's visit to Adonael's temple promised to be one of the least pleasant tasks he'd ever had to perform, but perform it he would.

The city came awake as he walked. People emerged from their homes and the smell of fresh bread filled the air as he passed a bakery. A blacksmith pounded metal into shape, but Danny didn't pause long enough to see what he was making. All in all, things seemed perfectly peaceful.

Ten minutes after he set out, Danny reached the city center. The government building wasn't much bigger than the Adventurers' Guild and as far as he could tell, it hadn't opened yet. Branik's temple looked like all the others he'd seen: a stone fortress with an inverted sword above the door and two guards on duty outside.

Following the road that circled the government building,

he arrived at the Goddess's temple next. The plain white stone building had little in the way of decorations yet somehow felt more welcoming than any of the other temples. No doubt some magic or simply Danny's positive past interactions with the clergy generated the good vibes.

At the third temple... He let out a breath. The golden halo over the door marked it as Adonael's. Like the Goddess's temple, it was built of white stone, but it resembled a fortress with nothing welcoming about it. Of course, that was probably all in his head.

Whatever the case, he pushed the door open, steeled himself, and entered a little vestibule between the entrance and the chapel. Finding no priest on duty, he tried the chapel door. It opened easily, so Danny continued inside. In the chapel, a priest crouched as he polished the wooden pews with a rag. He looked up when Danny entered and his face went as pale as his white robe. A disappointing reaction, but not unexpected.

"You can't be here," the priest said. "Sir Hugh went to meet you outside the city."

"He did meet me," Danny said. "A bunch of knights attacked me like common brigands, which is not what you would expect from the holy defenders of Adonael's faith. I dealt with them accordingly. Despite my distaste for their behavior, we did speak briefly beforehand. Hugh seemed like an honorable man tasked with carrying out a dishonorable mission."

"There can be no higher honor than performing a quest commanded by Lady Adonael."

"As the one who they attacked, I fear my perspective on the matter is somewhat different. In any case, I asked Hugh to tell her not to send any more good men to their deaths. I doubt she'll listen, but I'm going to tell you as well: if your faith wants to go to war with me, I'll level every temple I can find and bury every priest in the rubble, starting with you."

Danny found an empty space in front of the altar and opened his storage. One by one, he dragged the knights' bodies out and laid them on the floor in a neat row.

When he finished, he said, "They were good men and deserve a proper burial. Don't make me come back here. It won't end well for you."

"Do you have any idea of the size of Adonael's faith?" the priest asked. "Even you can't fight us all. Why don't you just do as you're commanded? Obeying the mandates of Heaven is every mortal's duty."

"You might be right," Danny said. "I don't know how big your faith is, but I do know there are six fewer members now. How many do you think she's willing to sacrifice to stop me? I am as determined to complete my mission as you are to obey your mistress. Neither you, nor your knights, nor anyone else you send after me will receive mercy. If I have to build a road of corpses to reach my destination, I will."

He took three steps forward, standing practically nose to nose with the trembling priest. "You know I'm from another world, correct?"

The priest nodded.

"Well, on my world, we have a saying: 'Fuck around and find out.' Sir Hugh and his men found out. Keep that in mind."

So saying, Danny stalked out of the temple. He doubted his warning would amount to much, but at least he'd tried to find a peaceful solution.

Putting the unpleasantness at Adonael's temple behind him, Danny made his way back toward the Adventurers' Guild. He wanted to gather more information about the drakes that lived in the forest. He didn't know if the information would be relevant, but his military experience had taught him to gather as much intel as possible before entering enemy territory. Danny really should've taken care of this yesterday, but he'd been tired, hungry, and eager to find a room for the night.

He turned down a street and paused. Two buildings down on the right stood a three-story dark stone structure marked with a sign featuring a book and a wand. It had to be the local Wizards' Guild. That might be a better place to do research. At the very least, it was on his way.

A few strides brought him to the front door. When he tried the handle, it didn't budge. Danny knocked and took out his Wizards' Guild badge. A few seconds later, a sour-faced man dressed in a crimson robe opened the door and glared at him. "We're not open to the public."

Danny held up his badge. "I'm a member and I'd like to do some research on the local drake population before heading out to the forest. This seemed like the best place to do so."

"Indeed it is." The wizard moved aside to let Danny enter. "I apologize for my rude greeting. You didn't look like a wizard at first glance."

Danny stepped into the entry area and closed the door. "No problem. Technically I'm an arcane knight, so I can see why you'd make that mistake. Do a lot of nonmembers try to come in?"

"Not a lot, but enough that it gets annoying. Are you an adventurer as well?"

Danny nodded. "Their guild was my next stop, but I

spotted this place and thought I might have better luck. The truth is, I know very little about drakes in general. Going into the forest this ignorant struck me as unwise."

The doorman finally smiled. "You have no idea how refreshing your attitude is. I started out as an adventurer as well and the number of people willing to charge forward without any idea of what they might encounter is beyond depressing. Personally, I think it explains in large part the high number of losses the guild faces. I'm Howard, by the way. Welcome to the Scale City Wizards' Guild."

"Ronin, and thank you for the welcome. I've only been an adventurer for about a year but many of the people I've met during that time were quite cautious. Given the danger, I'm surprised the locals are as cavalier as you make them sound."

"I shouldn't say this, but the truth is, Guild Master Mugg encourages aggressive exploration of the forest since it brings him the highest profits. He emphasizes that the Goddess's priests will heal anyone who gets hurt for free. What he doesn't mention is that you have to make it back alive to be healed. Given the damage a drake can inflict with a single strike, far too many don't."

"What does the Wizards' Guild master think about it?"

Howard lowered his voice and leaned closer. "Since we're the ultimate buyer for most drake parts, he doesn't complain lest Mugg decide to raise prices. The Adventurers' Guild has an effective monopoly on them after all."

"I was wondering about that. Can I sell any scales I find directly to you?"

"Technically, yes. As a member in good standing, you can sell to us, but I'll warn you that if Mugg finds out, he won't take it well. And he has a team of alpha elite adventurers who deal with any troublemakers."

Danny frowned. "Deal with troublemakers? Won't the rest of the guild members get pissed if their leader is killing their fellow adventurers?"

"There's no proof. So many are killed by the drakes that no one notices if one more group goes missing in the forest. It's not like they're getting knifed in the streets."

That was kind of clever in an evil sort of way. If he had a chance, Danny might have to do something about them. "Thanks for the warning. Could you show me to the library? I'd like to begin."

"Of course, please follow me. I fear that out here, far from real civilization, our collection isn't terribly impressive. However, we do have a comprehensive section on drakes and their use in various magical research applications." Howard led him around the counter that blocked access to the rest of the building and deeper into the guild.

Happily, they kept their modest library on the first floor. About a hundred books lined two bookshelves, and four tables surrounded by chairs provided places for members to sit and read. Danny had the place to himself at the moment, which suited him fine.

"I believe you'll want to start with *Drakes and Their Anatomy*," Howard said. "It's a good overview of all the species we've encountered, along with their abilities and weaknesses."

"Sounds perfect," Danny said.

"Pick a table and I'll grab it for you."

Danny settled at the nearest one. The chair had a nice, cushioned seat which would be great if he ended up doing a long stretch of research. Howard hadn't made the best first impression, but he didn't seem like a bad guy after all.

"Here you go." Howard set a blessedly thin leather-bound

book in front of him. "You know the rule, right? Guild books aren't allowed out of the library."

"I remember. Thanks again for all your help."

"That's what I'm here for. Just leave this or any other book you take out on the desk when you're finished. I'll put them back in the right spot." With a final nod, Howard left him alone to read.

Danny flipped open the first page and grinned when he found everything written in Common. He'd gotten his fill of using the translation spell in Elfhome.

The first chapter covered the basics. Drakes fell into two categories: lesser and greater. The primary distinctions were intelligence and whether or not they could fly. Lesser drakes resembled giant monitor lizards but were still smart and capable of various types of breath attacks. Greater drakes looked like Merrok, came in various colors, were incredibly smart and strong, and, the book emphasized, should be avoided.

While Danny considered that generally good advice, he still hoped to find a drake willing to speak with him about the ether pool. If anyone could guide him to it, surely it would be someone who lived in the forest. Of course, the ether pool most likely attracted the drakes to the area in the first place and increased their breeding rate, so they might not be pleased with his plan to destroy it.

He kept reading, focusing on the drakes' powers and how their coloration indicated what sort of magic they wielded. He found all the information in the book interesting and valuable. It took him about an hour to read the entire thing.

When he finished, Danny stood and stretched before walking over to the bookshelf. He knew all he ever wanted to about drakes. Time to try and find some information about the forest itself.

Thankfully, the spines were labeled with the books' titles, allowing him to get a rough idea of the subjects they covered. Most dealt with magical applications for drake parts as well as the plants growing in the forest. He grabbed one on rare plants and flipped it open. There were a few notes on where the target species generally grew, but none mentioned locations more than fifty miles deep into the forest. Surely someone had explored deeper than that; it was less than a tenth of the way to the center.

He put that book back and kept looking. One called *Legends of the Forest* caught his eye. On the first page, the author had written a warning stating that all the stories included in the book came from a translation of an old Elvish tome and should be treated as unconfirmed rumors, which the reader relied on at their own risk. Rumors may or may not prove useful, but an Elvish source made Danny optimistic.

Taking the book back to his seat, he settled in to read some more. The author, or perhaps the translator, followed no particular narrative structure. Instead, it seemed to be a collection of random anecdotes. They mentioned hidden villages deep in the forest, a castle built by an eccentric half-elf obsessed with drakes, and a legendary queen of the forest. Despite the sparse details, he found the stories intriguing. All of them seemed to take place far deeper in the forest than anyone had explored recently.

He sighed and closed the book. Maybe some of it was true and maybe none of it was but given that he sought an elf-blood facility, the idea of a half-elf living in the area seemed well within the realm of possibility. Hopefully the

Reaper had chased him off with the rest of the elf-bloods. Danny didn't need a half-elf wizard, likely stronger than Lyra, hanging around looking to cause trouble. He'd have enough problems with the drakes.

Danny left the books on his table and retraced his steps to the entry area. Howard sat behind the counter, reading a book of his own. He looked up when Danny approached.

"Did you find what you were looking for?"

Danny grinned. "I didn't really know what I was looking for, but I did find a bunch of interesting information. Do you know why there are no details about the deeper areas of the forest? As best I can tell, there's nothing about the areas more than fifty miles in. Given the size of it, there has to be a ton of useful material in there."

"I'm sure there is," Howard said. "But no one who has tried to go deeper than that has come back alive. I can't remember the last time I heard about a group attempting to delve that deep. All the adventurers basically consider it a death sentence."

"That's not very encouraging. What happens? Do the drakes get stronger the deeper in you go?"

Howard nodded. "Exactly. And they get more aggressive too, since they don't want to give up their territory."

Danny ran a hand over his bare scalp. Sounded like he was really stepping into it this time. "I appreciate all your help. I'm off to the Adventurers' Guild."

"Be careful," Howard said.

Danny would certainly do his best. He threw a final wave over his shoulder and marched out the door.

A block away, he reached the Adventurers' Guild and found the common room empty save for a burly man in a too-small green tunic and brown trousers, who occupied a small table in the corner. A scar ran along his cheek, up the side of his skull, and through his dark hair, leaving a bald streak. Danny had no idea what might've caused a scar like that and hoped he wouldn't find out.

He stepped over to the job board and scanned the list of permanently sought items, comparing it to what he'd learned at the Wizards' Guild. The plants were categorized based on how deep they supposedly grew in the forest, which also served as a reasonable proxy for the danger of collecting them. It was strange that all the scales had the same price.

"Ronin!"

He turned to see Erin waving to him from the counter. He smiled and ambled over. "Morning. Quiet today."

She nodded. "Everyone's gone out hunting. I figured you would've gotten an early start too."

"I swung by the Wizards' Guild to do some research. I knew far too little about the forest to just charge in. That's a good way to end up in trouble. It's best to take your time and do it right. The drakes aren't going anywhere after all."

"Bah!" The scarred man pushed away from his table and stalked over, towering a good six inches over Danny. "Research is for wizards. An adventurer needs to see things with his own eyes. What good is book learning compared to that?"

"Well," Danny said. "Knowing what to look for and having at least some idea of what your potential prey can do seems like the minimum any prudent hunter would want to learn. Given the lack of information, that's about all there is to learn in any case. I mean, who'd think a lesser earth drake could spit acid? What does earth have to do with acid? That's the sort of surprise that might get a man killed. Being an adventurer requires risk; I accepted that when I joined. But there are smart risks and stupid ones."

The big man narrowed his eyes. "You calling me stupid, boy?"

"I'm not calling you anything, but charging in blind and ignorant is undoubtedly stupid. Whether you agree with me or not doesn't change my opinion at all."

The big man snorted. "The Adventurers' Guild is no place for cowards. You won't last long."

With that, he stomped off deeper into the building.

Danny turned back to Erin. "Charming fellow."

"Guild Master Mugg has a bit of a rough personality," Erin said. "But it's necessary to run things out in the middle of nowhere."

She added that last bit as if trying to convince herself.

"That was the guild master?" Danny could hardly believe it. "He should be the one warning everyone to be careful. Does he want his members to end up dead?"

She didn't answer and refused to meet his gaze. That told Danny a lot. Combined with what he'd learned from Howard, his opinion of Mugg dropped even further. Hopefully, he wasn't cut from the same cloth as Berend. One corrupt guild master in a lifetime was enough.

CHAPTER 4

Danny strode through the city's lone gate, past disinterested guards who barely turned to look at him, and out into the noon sun. It shone bright and warm and he took a deep breath. He couldn't imagine a nicer day to visit a giant forest filled with carnivorous drakes.

They'd built the city a good forty miles from the forest or about a half day's run at his best pace. Despite the late start, he should reach the outskirts before dark. He still had no idea how people handled camping. It had to be sketchy sleeping in the forest, but by the same token, a few hours of exploring wouldn't let you cover much ground.

Well, he'd figure it out when he arrived. Guild Master Mugg might not have been the most pleasant fellow Danny had ever met, but he had a point about needing to see some things for yourself. Danny resolved not to think about the man any further and infused his body with ether.

He kicked the ground and set off down the rough dirt road at a magically enhanced run. He vaguely noted the scattered footprints of previous adventurers as he ate up the miles. He didn't see a single hoofprint in the bunch; no doubt any sort of animal would be good for nothing beyond drake bait.

The grasslands and low scrub became little more than a blur as he rushed by. Hours passed at his now-familiar, ground-devouring pace. Danny ran in a sort of trance, aware of little beyond putting one foot in front of the other, his magical senses alert for any approaching life force or source of corruption. Aside from plants and ordinary animals, he sensed nothing around for miles.

Eventually he spotted a group on the road ahead. They had to be the last to leave before him. He soon closed the distance and grinned as they stared in surprise. They looked young, too young to be heading somewhere as dangerous as the forest.

Danny shook his head as soon as the thought formed. They all looked older than his host body. They bore weapons and armor of decent quality at least. Not that any of it would stand up to a drake's claws. Hopefully their stealth skills were on point.

Danny quickly left the gaping rookies behind. He couldn't worry about their futures. All adventurers made a choice to accept the risks when they entered this line of work. He'd hope things worked out for them and focus on his own mission.

As dusk fell, colossal trees jutting into the orange-and-red sky came into view. They reminded Danny of Elfhome. Hopefully he wouldn't find any demons to go with the drakes he'd have to deal with. Unless they were as friendly as Riko, in which case he wouldn't mind.

Flickering campfires dotted a clearing a couple of miles

out from the forest's edge. Four groups of adventurers had arrived and set up camp for the night. The clearing looked well-used. It was probably the last safe place to rest before entering the forest.

Danny focused on the ether. A powerful ward shimmered around the clearing's perimeter. Had the Adventurers' Guild arranged it? Having met Mugg, Danny had his doubts, but maybe some previous guild master had been more generous.

Not an especially difficult hurdle to clear.

Danny released his enhancements and approached the campground at a walk. The savory aroma of cooking food filled the air. He hadn't stopped during his run, and Danny wanted to set up his own camp and make something for dinner.

As he debated where to pitch his tent, a gruff, familiar voice said, "Hi there, Ronin! Why don't you come share our fire and a bowl of soup?"

Evard sat sprawled by a crackling fire with an iron pot bubbling merrily in front of him. Steam curled up from the pot, carrying the mouthwatering scent of herbs and meat.

Danny hesitated. He couldn't figure out Evard's game. Then again, having spent so much time around sketchy people, Danny might be assuming the worst. Until Evard did something to make it clear he had an agenda, Danny would take him at face value.

"Thanks, I think I'll take you up on that. It smells wonderful."

Danny sat by the fire, the heat pleasant as the evening chill settled in. Up close, the soup smelled even more delicious, thick with chunks of potato, carrot, and some kind of white meat bubbling in the broth.

He pulled a bowl and spoon out of his pack. Danny kept

the basics handy to avoid sharing the secret of his magical storage with strangers. Evard ladled out a generous portion into his bowl.

"Tuck in. It's going to be a long few days in the forest."

Danny silently activated a detect poison spell and when it confirmed the soup contained nothing dangerous, he took a bite. It tasted better than it smelled. Whatever skill he might have as a team leader, Danny didn't know, but if adventuring didn't work out, Evard had a future as a cook.

Eating quietly, Danny took a peek at the other members of Evard's Blade. They sat hunched over their own meals, eyeing Danny with expressions ranging from disinterest to suspicion. The latter came strictly from Brand. Danny had no idea what he'd done to earn the man's ire, but clearly he'd pissed the guy off somehow.

He focused on his food, savoring the rich flavor of the soup as it warmed him from the inside out.

Halfway through his meal, Evard said, "I didn't think you'd make it this far today."

"I'm good at physical enhancement magic. This was a pretty easy run for me. I assume that's how you guys did it. A forty-mile run is no joke without magic."

"All credit to our wizard. I can't use any magic myself."

Danny always felt kind of bad for people unable to wield the ether, which included most of them. Magic made things so convenient.

"Best enjoy the food and a good night's sleep," Evard said. "Once you enter the forest, both are hard to come by."

"I was thinking about that," Danny said. "It must take a pretty heavy-duty ward to discourage a drake."

"That's for sure. We sleep lightly and in shifts; it wears you out in a hurry. If we can manage a week or so in the forest, that's a lot. Odds are you won't even see a drake, but the constant stress is exhausting. Can't imagine how you'll manage on your own."

"I'll be okay." Danny finished off the last of his soup then cleaned the bowl and spoon with magic. "Thanks for the meal and good luck tomorrow."

"You too, lad. Should you change your mind in the morning, you're welcome to join us."

Danny nodded his thanks and moved a short distance away to set up his one-person tent. Despite the guild ward in place, he took the time to lay his own protective barrier. He made it non-lethal just in case someone stumbled into it on their way to the bushes.

That done, he settled in for the night. His thoughts drifted as he tried to fall asleep. The forest should be interesting, though hopefully not too interesting. He'd make his way straight to the center since he assumed he'd find the ether pool in that general vicinity. At least he planned to start looking there. He would, as always, adjust his plan as he went.

Assuming the drakes didn't adjust it for him.

CHAPTER 5

Danny slipped silently out of his little tent and stood in the pitch-black campsite. No one else had risen yet and that suited him perfectly since he had no desire for conversation, or more accurately, no interest in answering questions about his plans. Too many people were too curious for his comfort.

It didn't take long to break down his camp and, after a quick breakfast of dried fruit and bread, he crept out of the campsite. The combination of darkvision and stealth field made it easy to avoid disturbing the snoring adventurers sprawled in little clumps around the clearing.

The two-mile hike to the forest's edge didn't take long, but it did give the sun a chance to peek over the horizon. As the pale dawn light filtered through scattered clouds, Danny paused beside one of the towering evergreens. Even this far from the ether pool, the tree measured a good eight feet in diameter and probably several hundred feet tall. It would likely yield enough lumber to build a fair-sized house.

Danny narrowed his eyes and focused on the ether.

Specifically, how it interacted with the trees. He found traces deep in the heartwood. Not much, but enough to prove the trees' growth had a supernatural element. This made him more confident that he would find the ether pool eventually. He'd been nearly on top of it before detecting the flow at the crystal mine.

No sense delaying. Danny squared his shoulders and marched between two of the huge trunks. A bed of fallen orange needles covered the forest floor. With his stealth field running, he didn't disturb them. No one would be able to follow or detect him as long as the magic remained active, exactly as he wanted.

The canopy stretched overhead like a vast green ceiling, casting mottled shadows over everything. The dense shadows kept the undergrowth to a minimum, leaving the forest floor largely bare, which made walking easy.

But the trunks, ancient and gnarled, crowded close together, far too close for a normal forest, forcing him to weave between them at a maddeningly slow pace. If he moved faster than a quick jog, he risked a face-first collision with unyielding bark. The pace annoyed him, but he tamped down his frustration. Losing focus here would not end well.

Time seemed to warp and stretch, minutes blurring into hours as Danny jogged on. Normal animals lived in the trees; birds chirped, and squirrels chattered, all blissfully unaware of Danny's presence. The Forest of Drakes had little in common with Elfhome. The first and most obvious difference was the lack of corruption. Danny appreciated the low odds of running into a random demon as he searched. Of course, the possibility of encountering a random drake made up for it.

Around midday he paused to rest. He'd covered maybe

ten or twelve miles since dawn. A decent clip, but not nearly fast enough to suit him. At this rate, it would take weeks, maybe even a month, to reach the heart of the forest.

He leaned against a mossy trunk, dug a strip of jerky out of his pack, and tore into it. There had to be a way to give it more flavor. Chewing mechanically, he considered his options for speeding his journey. Picking up the pace would mean sacrificing caution and Danny hadn't gotten comfortable enough in the forest for that. Maybe—

A scream brought his musings to an abrupt halt. Panicked shouts preceded a roar that shook the trees.

Sounded like someone had run into the local wildlife.

He hesitated for a moment. It was really none of his business.

Danny sighed. Who was he kidding? Muttering a curse aimed firmly at himself, he shoved the rest of the jerky into his mouth and took off at a run, weaving through the trees toward the sounds of battle.

A few hundred yards later, he burst into a small clearing and skidded to a halt. Three battered adventurers faced off against a massive, brown-scaled drake, their weapons—looking far too inadequate for the enemy in front of them—steady in their hands. A fourth person lay in two bloody pieces on the ground, his lifeless eyes staring at nothing.

The drake hadn't noticed him yet. Good, it looked like his stealth field worked as well against drakes as it did against everything else. He hadn't been sure, despite his relative confidence. The brown scales and lack of wings marked it as a lesser mud drake. According to his research, it should be vulnerable to lightning.

Danny thrust out his hand and sent a crackling bolt slamming into the beast's hindquarters, well clear of the desperate adventurers.

The drake staggered, a howl of pain mingling with the stink of burnt flesh.

His attack canceled his stealth field, revealing Danny to everyone present.

"Get out of there!" Danny yelled at the stunned adventurers as he readied another blast.

His shout cleared their rattled brains and they hastened to scramble clear, stumbling over roots and rocks in their haste to escape.

As soon as they moved out of the way, Danny loosed another bolt, this time aiming for the drake's chest.

The spell struck home, sending the beast reeling.

But not dead. For a moment, it looked as though it might attack. Its eyes blazed with fury as it glared at Danny.

Happily the drake thought better of it and fled before Danny had to blast it a third time. Its crashing retreat through the trees quickly grew more distant.

Danny didn't relax until it moved beyond earshot.

With the area reasonably secure, he hurried over to the survivors, who had collapsed to their knees behind a fallen tree trunk. All three bore wounds, though none appeared life-threatening. Bloodstains covered their torn clothing, now barely more than rags. If they'd been on Earth, Danny would've suggested they buy a lottery ticket.

Kneeling beside them, he sent ether charged with divine energy into them. Their wounds began to knit together at an accelerated rate. Pained grimaces gave way to relief.

When he finished healing them, a man perhaps ten years Danny's senior, who seriously needed a change of clothes and a bath, said, "Thank you. We'd have been dead if you hadn't shown up."

Danny shook his head, his expression grim. "Just dumb luck I was in the area. What happened?"

"It's more than luck. Most adventurers wouldn't jump into a fight with a drake to save strangers." The man blew out a breath. "We were collecting rare herbs and got so caught up in the excitement of finally finding something valuable that we let our guard down. It was stupid, but after days of searching, no sleep, and little food, it was such a relief. Bloody drake snuck up on us before we knew what was happening."

He shook his head, his eyes haunted. "It's a miracle the damn thing didn't kill us all. We should have been—I should've been more careful. I've been working this miserable forest for three years. I know better! And now Gail's dead. I was so damn eager to make a score."

Danny felt bad for the guy, but despite his considerable power, he could do nothing for the dead and any words he offered would ring hollow.

The man—Danny assumed he served as the group's leader—reached into his pack and pulled out a small bundle of herbs. "Please, take this as a token of our gratitude. It's the least we can do after what you did for us."

Danny glanced at the other survivors, but they weren't paying the least attention to the discussion. They had the vacant, thousand-yard stare of people who'd faced death and lived to tell the tale.

"Keep it," Danny said. "Your team earned it and then some. Are you good to make it back to the campsite on your own? I can't backtrack."

"We'll be fine, sir. Thank you again for saving us and for

your generosity. If the Glorious Raiders can ever do anything for you in the future, you need only ask. My name is Piers Wyn, and I won't forget this until my dying day."

"Ronin." Danny held out his hand and they shook. "Take care of yourselves."

Goodbyes said, Danny moved out of sight and reactivated his stealth field. Hopefully he could make it through the rest of the day without running into anything else that might want to eat him.

CHAPTER 6

Danny crouched on a massive, gnarled branch and scanned the forest floor for any signs of movement. The poor line of sight made the forest a nightmare; the trees blocked everything. In a clear section, he might see forty yards.

After three days of marching deeper into the Forest of Drakes, he figured he'd covered about fifty miles, placing him around the edge of the unexplored zone. Or so he guessed. Nothing marked the border and his zigzagging path made calculating distances with any precision impossible. Moreover, one part of the forest looked pretty much the same as the next.

Regardless, he had made some progress and that pleased him.

Since parting ways with the Glorious Raiders, he hadn't encountered a single drake or anything more threatening than a passing boar. Evard had told him they rarely saw drakes, and it seemed he'd been right. No doubt Danny's stealth field helped tip the odds in his favor.

He leapt to the next tree and found a sturdy crook between two thick branches that looked perfect for stringing up his hammock. He'd bought it on a whim in Discourt and kept it in storage. It should be just the thing to keep him off the ground while he slept, thus making him at least a little safer.

Danny ate a meager supper of hard cheese and bread. He hadn't dared to make a fire and cooking with magic after maintaining the stealth field all day didn't appeal to him.

A deep, rumbling bellow echoed through the darkening woods. He froze, a piece of cheese halfway to his mouth, and listened. He couldn't tell how far away the drake might be, but it was far enough to prevent Danny from sensing its life force.

Based on the deep, bass rumble, he figured a larger-than-average drake had loosed the roar. Probably one significantly bigger than the mud drake. Not an encouraging thought. Danny had no way to know what type he'd heard, but if it found him, he'd be in for another fight. He finished his uninspiring meal and brushed the crumbs off his tunic.

He'd need to keep an extra-sharp eye out tomorrow. Hopefully he'd sense the drake before he stumbled across it. The book he'd read said little about their magical abilities beyond the types of breath attacks they used. That seemed like the sort of thing someone should study properly, assuming you could find some drakes willing to cooperate.

He grinned at the ridiculous thought.

As full darkness fell over the forest, Danny settled into his hammock and set a lethal ward. Any unwelcome visitor passing by in the night and thinking of messing with him would get a nasty surprise.

A light breeze rustled the dense canopy, carrying the

earthy scents of moss and decaying needles. Danny closed his eyes and tried not to think about what tomorrow would bring.

Nothing troubled him during the night, and after a breakfast every bit as bland as the previous evening's supper, Danny set out. He carried the ethersword in his right hand but didn't activate it.

He'd barely hit the ground and taken a step when a tremor rippled through the dirt. A moment later, the earth exploded in a shower of rock as a massive shape burst forth.

The drake, its scales a mottled green, reared up before him, jaws gaping to reveal vicious fangs dripping with acid.

"Shit!" Danny dove to the side, narrowly avoiding a snap of its jaws that would've left him in two pieces.

He rolled, evading talons that cut foot-deep grooves in the dirt.

Danny sprang to his feet and ignited the ethersword, just in time to hack a deep line in the drake's left claw.

It roared and snatched its leg back.

The beast studied him with dark-yellow, far-too-intelligent eyes.

It had to be fifty feet long, including its whip-like tail. The lesser earth drake—Danny recognized it from the description he'd read—resembled an oversized monitor lizard. One that spit acid and apparently tunneled through the ground like a gopher. The book hadn't mentioned that last ability, though with a name like earth drake, it didn't come as a huge surprise.

The drake circled left, and Danny matched it, moving

right. Even lesser drakes were supposed to be smart, maybe if he tried talking to it they wouldn't have to fight.

"I'm not interested in your territory," Danny said. "What do you say we just go our separate ways?"

The drake roared and charged, the ground shaking beneath its claws.

Danny leapt aside at the last second, raking his blade across its flank, cutting another deep groove and drawing a pained shriek.

"Seriously, I don't want to fight you. I'm just trying to find an ether pool. You don't know where it is by any chance?"

The drake spun with more agility than something its size should possess.

Its tail lashed out, sending Danny flying twenty feet into a tree. His personal shield absorbed the worst of the impact, but it still hurt.

Okay, no more talking to the stupid lizard. If the drake wanted to die, he'd grant its wish.

Danny pushed away from the tree and charged at maximum speed right at the drake.

It tried another tail swipe.

Danny leapt over it, his ether-powered legs propelling him onto its back. He drove the ethersword in up to the hilt.

The drake roared and thrashed, sending him flying and ripping the cut open wider.

Somehow the drake stayed on its feet despite the blood rushing down its side. An impressive show of toughness, but it should bleed out before too long.

Not that he planned to wait. Danny channeled ether through the mithril hilt of his sword and launched a massive lightning bolt.

The spell slammed into the drake's neck, nearly severing its head and finally sending it crashing to the ground where it lay still, its final fragments of life force slipping away.

He kicked it a couple of times to make sure, then let his enhancements fade and deactivated the ethersword. Though no match for Merrok, the earth drake had put up a pretty good fight. He understood now why adventurers didn't want to venture this deep into the forest.

Danny looked around the site of their battle. They'd done a good job ripping up the place. His gaze settled on the dead drake. He didn't know how much it would sell for, but at a minimum it should fit in storage. It would be worth the effort to bring it back just to see the looks on everyone's faces.

But he'd deal with that later. Right now, he needed to rest. The drake's territory should be safe for the moment. A hot breakfast before setting out sounded like just the thing. The cheese and dried meat hadn't really filled him up.

Once he made up his mind, Danny had a couple of sausages sizzling over a fire in short order. The delicious smell made his mouth water. Once the skin finished crisping up, he set his back to a tree and started eating.

Hopefully he wouldn't have to fight too many more drakes. If a lesser drake was this tough, a greater drake would really push him—especially since he didn't have the hero's armor anymore. Heaven forbid he encountered one stronger than Merrok.

He gave himself two hours of extra rest, then got underway after loading the drake carcass into his storage. It took up about a third of the space, but he still had plenty of room left should he run into any more of them.

CHAPTER 7

Danny hiked, untroubled, through the Forest of Drakes. A soft breeze carried the scent of spruce and cedar. After yesterday's battle, he appreciated the peace. He attributed his quiet travel to still being in the earth drake's territory. He didn't know for sure, but something that big had to have a sizable hunting ground.

Sweat trickled down Danny's brow as he pressed onward at a quick jog. Despite the shadows, it felt like summer today. He didn't know this world's calendar very well, but back home it would've been June by now. After freezing and slogging through the wilderness north of Elfhome, he welcomed the heat.

He stopped to wipe the sweat from his brow. Might be time for a quick lunch break. He expanded his senses to make sure nothing dangerous lurked nearby. To his considerable surprise, he sensed a faint but unmistakable solitary human presence.

Who the hell would be out here? No adventurer would

risk exploring this deep into the forest. He was the only one crazy enough for that. Curiosity got the better of him and he veered off course, following the mysterious life force.

About a hundred yards later, Danny stepped into a clearing and stared at the least likely thing imaginable. Someone had chained a gorgeous young woman to a thick wooden post. Her arms strained above her drooping head. With only her long dark hair for clothes, her flawless bronze skin was on full display. Danny had seen his share of strange things since coming to this world, but a naked damsel in distress straight out of a cheesy fantasy novel? That was a first.

Right, focus. He approached slowly, hands out to the side in a gesture of peace. His eyes did their best to ignore the sights on display. Sadly, his best efforts proved woefully inadequate, and he kept glancing at the curves before him.

The girl watched him approach, her eyes wide with panic. She looked left and right but had nowhere to go, not chained up like that. If he ever got his hands on whoever did this to her, he'd happily wring their neck.

"Easy now. I'm not going to hurt you," Danny said, keeping his voice low and soothing. "What's your name?"

She licked her lips, and the chains rattled as she shifted. "Liana. Please, you must flee before it's too late! The great one will be here before long."

Danny scratched his head. "Great one? If you're talking about the lesser earth drake, don't worry, I killed it yesterday. There's no way another one has already shown up to take its place. We should still be safe here. For a little while anyway."

"The great ones are invincible," Liana said.

"No, they're tough, but hardly invincible." He frowned. Come to think of it, for most people, a drake of any sort came pretty close to being invincible. He couldn't blame her for not believing him. "Here, I'll show you."

Danny opened his storage, reached in, and dragged the drake's head and a foot of neck into view. "See, it's dead. You're safe. Now let's get you out of those manacles, and then you can tell me the whole story."

She let out a little squeal and the blood drained from her face at the sight of the drake's head. Yeah, maybe that had been a bit excessive. But at least now she knew for sure it wouldn't show up and eat her.

Danny crafted a key out of ether and used it to pop open the crude padlocks holding her manacles closed. Liana rubbed her chafed wrists, wincing. The sight pissed him off all over again.

A bit of divine ether healed the abrasions. "Better?"

She stared at her now perfectly smooth skin in wonder. "Yes, thank you."

"Good." Danny stuck his head into his storage space and rummaged around in the trunk where he kept his spare clothes. Bingo—an extra tunic, one he hadn't worn yet. It should be plenty big enough for such a petite woman. He reached back and offered it to her. "Try this on."

Shoes were going to be a bigger problem. He had an extra set of boots, but they wouldn't work for her; they'd look like clown shoes and be clumsy. A moment later, he found a sheet of canvas. Maybe if he cut it into strips, they could wrap her feet. Not exactly ideal, but better than the alternative.

He backed out with the canvas and his ethersword in hand. A few swipes of the white blade transformed the canvas into tan mummy wrappings. That done, he turned back to Liana.

The tunic worked as a sort of minidress, with the hem

reaching about midthigh. Suzy used to wear his t-shirts like that. Hottest thing he ever saw. Liana pulled the style off quite nicely as well.

"I appreciate your kindness," she said, "but you shouldn't have saved me. The Master of Drakes will be furious."

"I don't know who that is," Danny said. "But anyone who would order an innocent young woman fed to a drake is a villain in my book. If he tries to cause me trouble, I'll deal with him the same way I did his pet."

Liana shook her head. "The Master of Drakes is a powerful sorcerer. He brought our ancestors to our village generations ago, and he protects us from the great ones. In exchange, we provide a sacrifice every five years. It's a small price to pay for a life of safety."

She seemed remarkably content with the idea of dying for her people, and not an easy death either. Getting eaten by a drake had to be a painful way to go. The more Danny thought about the situation, the less sense it made. One person every five years wouldn't make a dent in a drake's diet, and he sensed no magic in the area that might bind the beast.

No, he'd walked into something strange. Fortunately it didn't concern him, at least not at the moment.

"Let's put that aside for now," Danny said. "We'll wrap up your feet then I can escort you home. Your parents, I'm sure, will be glad to see you safe and sound."

She bit her lip for a moment, then said, "They won't. I'm already dead in the eyes of the village. It's a great honor to be chosen as the sacrifice; my family will be held in high regard. If I show up now, they're more likely to kill me as a heretic than welcome me home."

Well, shit. If he left her alone, the girl wouldn't last long out here. And taking her back to her village sounded like a bad idea if the people there meant her harm.

"Okay, change of plans. I'll bring you to Scale, that's the name of a nearby city, instead." The trip back would take Danny significantly out of his way, but it'd give him a chance to sell the drake and buy some supplies, so it wouldn't be a complete waste of time. Helping Liana was also the right thing to do. "We'll set you up with an apartment, some new clothes, and a proper pair of shoes. Do you have any skills?"

"Just the basics everyone learns. I can cook, sew a little, tend goats and chickens, and weed the garden. Why are you doing this for me? I'm a total stranger."

"I'm a sucker for a woman in trouble. If I walked away and left you alone out here, I'd never be able to live with myself. What do you say we wrap your feet up and get out of here?"

"Okay. One question first. What is your name?"

"Right, sorry. I'm Ronin, pleasure to meet you, Liana."

Calum Thorne, better known to his followers as the Master of Drakes, strode into a particular clearing in the Forest of Drakes. His green robe swished around his legs as his gaze darted about. Even for him, the forest held many dangers. You underestimated it at your peril.

Despite his caution, Calum was in a good mood. Sacrifice day for Village Three had arrived, and he wanted to collect the latest power source for his ritual as soon as possible. The spell neared completion and if heaven favored him, this sacrifice would complete the matrix. Two hundred years of work had brought him to this point, and he wanted to finish sooner rather than later.

In the center of the clearing, he found the sacrifice post empty. Calum narrowed his gray eyes. The manacles hung open as the metal chain clinked softly in the breeze.

Where was his sacrifice?

His lips twitched and twisted into a grimace as he cocked his head and listened. Only the warble of forest birds filled the air. He'd seldom beheld a more peaceful day. The villagers wouldn't dare forget. Not after over a century of unbroken obedience.

He walked to the post and ran a slim finger over the manacles. No blood or flecks of skin. She hadn't been taken by force or devoured by his lesser earth drake. The latter concerned him more than the former, as it would mean the beast had slipped the leash of his magic. A potentially alarming turn of events to be sure.

No, someone had released her. But who?

Calum's frown deepened. The villagers knew better than to defy him. It must have been one of the adventurers who spent so much time poking around his forest. He'd set a number of lesser drakes to guard the inner forest and prevent any interlopers from penetrating this deep. Apparently, someone had snuck past them. An impressive feat for a mere human.

Calum reached into the folds of his emerald robe and withdrew the Flute of Commanding Drakes. The silver instrument gleamed in the dappled sunlight, its sinuous curves mimicking the serpentine form of a drake. One of his ancestors, a half-elf of great magical ability, had crafted the flute before the fall of Elfhome.

He raised it to his lips and blew. The flute made no sound, but magic flowed out through the ether.

One minute passed. Then two.

And nothing. The lesser earth drake had to be around here. The flute had a range of a mile. The clever drake would know that sacrifice day had arrived and that Calum would be coming, which meant it should stay close.

Or so he'd ordered the cursed beast. First, his sacrifice was stolen and now his drake was defying its orders. What had once been a glorious day had turned into a nightmare.

Calum lowered the flute, a cold unease settling in the pit of his stomach. Something had gone very wrong in his forest. Jaw clenched, Calum marched out of the clearing toward Village Three. They would provide the answers he needed.

The crude collection of ramshackle huts lay only a mile from the clearing. Nothing troubled him on his walk save his own unquiet thoughts. Had someone come to oppose him after all this time? Some forgotten ally of the Forest Queen?

He dismissed the idea as soon as it formed. If she had such an ally, she would've called upon them long ago. No, she remained trapped and alone in her castle, just as she had been since Calum's half-elf ancestor bound her there.

Something else had appeared to trouble him. Whether better or worse, time would tell.

He emerged from the treeline and stalked toward the village. The humans scurried out of their huts. A shout went up and the people working the nearby fields came running.

Soon, all of them had prostrated themselves before him, trembling as his shadow fell across their bowed heads.

The mayor, a title far too lofty for the withered human, dared to glance up at Calum, his white beard trembling. "H-how may we serve you, Master?"

"The sacrifice," Calum snapped. "Where is she?"

The mayor's weathered face crinkled in confusion. "We brought Liana to the post at first light, as we are commanded. Was she not suitable for the great ones?"

Calum studied the man's face. His magic revealed no deceit in the mayor's words. At least the villagers remained loyal. Good, that eliminated one thing from his list of worries.

"She was taken," Calum said.

"By whom, Master?" the mayor asked.

Calum's lips thinned. "I don't know yet."

"Will another girl suffice? We judged Liana the most beautiful, but we have several others nearly as fine."

Calum considered for a moment, then shook his head. The contract required the village to provide one sacrifice every five years. They had upheld their end. His honor wouldn't allow him to take another of them, no matter the convenience.

"No," he said at last. "Someone dared to steal from me. They will be punished and the sacrifice recovered."

He spun on his heel and stalked away. He would find the thief. If it was an adventurer—and he failed to imagine anyone else who might be foolish enough to come here—then they must've taken Liana to Scale City.

Calum hated the place, full of so many humans with their stink and greed and stupidity. He'd visited several times decades ago to decide whether they threatened the forest. It hadn't taken long to confirm they didn't. Even the strongest among them wouldn't last a second against the weakest drake. They were insects nibbling around the edges of his beautiful forest.

Now it looked like one of those insects needed to be crushed.

CHAPTER 8

The towering stone walls of Scale appeared on the horizon an hour after noon. Everything looked peaceful from a distance. The many towers and their mounted ballistae no doubt played a large role in keeping it that way.

Danny hadn't expected to be back this fast, especially not traveling with a normal girl. But they'd discovered pretty quickly that if they wanted to make any progress, Danny needed to carry Liana. She weighed so little riding piggyback that, with his ether enhanced strength, he barely noticed her weight. Her chest pressed against his back, on the other hand, proved a constant distraction.

Luckily, despite his distracted state, they made it to the city safe and sound.

In fact, they hadn't encountered a single danger on the road. He didn't know why but he didn't plan to complain.

Danny stopped about two miles out from the city gate and set Liana down.

"Why are we stopping here?" she asked.

"One, it'll look less weird if you walk in on your own. Two, I need to do something before we arrive."

Danny opened his storage and grabbed the ethersword. Slowly and with maximum precision he sliced six scales off the drake carcass without damaging the other scales around them.

Liana watched with a little frown creasing her lips. "What are you doing?"

"Just testing a theory," Danny said. "Don't worry about it."

She nodded. "What's going to happen to me now? I don't know anyone in the city."

"I'm not sure yet. But we'll figure something out. I didn't bring you all this way just to leave you on your own with a fare-thee-well."

"Thank you, Ronin, for everything. I was sure I'd be dead long ago. I was even honored to die for my village, but after everything you told me, I can see that was wrong."

Everything about Liana's situation was wrong, he just hadn't figured out exactly how yet. That might be something he needed to look into when he got back to the forest.

Danny offered a wry inner smile. So much for just focusing on his mission.

"I'm glad to help." And he meant it. Danny took great pleasure in helping people. It's what he imagined he'd be doing when he joined the Marines. That it hadn't turned out the way he'd hoped had been... disappointing.

He tucked the scales into his pack and nodded toward the city gates. "Come on, let's find you something better to wear than my extra tunic and some strips of canvas."

She spun a little circle, giving him a full view of her very shapely legs. "I think it suits me, but some shoes would be nice."

When they reached the gate, the guards gave his guild card a quick look and Liana a longer one. He couldn't get mad at them. She was insanely easy to look at.

Inside, they made their way through the bustling streets until Danny spotted a general store, its weathered sign depicting a sack and hammer. A bell jangled when he pushed open the door. The earthy scent of leather and lye soap washed over him. Shelves stretched from floor to ceiling, crammed with all manner of goods: lanterns, rope coils, pickaxes, iron cookware… and bingo, a reasonable collection of clothes.

Liana gazed around in wonder, reaching out to stroke a bolt of colorful red yarn. "I've never seen so many things in one place before."

"You should see the shops in Discourt, they make this place look ordinary." Danny guided her over to a table covered with neatly folded women's clothing. Someone had even set up a privacy screen to let customers try on their purchases. "Pick out whatever you want. I'll wait by the counter."

He left her to make her selections and headed for the food aisle. Danny noticed on their way back that his supplies were getting a bit low. With all the space he had in storage, he saw no reason to risk running out, especially since nothing spoiled in there. He grabbed a string of dried sausage links and a cloth bag filled with rolls. Next came five pounds of bacon and a ten-pound bag of beans.

When his hands were full, he set the goods on the checkout counter where an old man, his face a mass of wrinkles and his head surround by a halo of white hair, gave him a serious look-see.

"Before you grab anything else, sonny, let's see your coin."

Danny put two of the local gold coins on the counter and the proprietor's eyes widened. "Righto, enjoy your shopping."

"Thanks." He went back to the food section and gathered enough to last, he hoped, three months. When he'd finished, Liana came to join him. She'd traded his tunic for a blue, knee-length dress and a pair of simple but sturdy leather shoes. "Looking good."

She smiled and her cheeks reddened. "Thank you. The shoes especially feel wonderful."

"I imagine so." He took his tunic and the strips of canvas back and stuffed them into his pack. "How much for everything, including the dress and shoes?"

The old man had been keeping track with a slate and chalk. He quickly added in Liana's selections and said, "Gonna need one more gold coin to go with the first two."

Danny set a third coin on the counter and the proprietor scooped up all of them.

"Pleasure doing business with you. Stop by Cobb's General Store anytime you need supplies. If you'll excuse me, I need to restock the food section." Without waiting for a reply, the old man—Cobb, Danny assumed—hurried off toward the back of the shop.

When he'd gone, Danny put his food into storage and led the way outside.

"Where to now?" Liana asked.

"The Temple of the Goddess. If this one is anything like the others I've visited, they should have some rooms available for people in distress. There's no one else I'd trust to keep you safe."

"Do you think the Master of Drakes will try to bring me back?" Her fear sent a tremor through her voice.

Danny set out for the temple. "I don't know enough about

him to say for sure one way or the other, but I'll feel better if you're somewhere secure. And not just because of him. A pretty girl like you, on your own in a rough city like this... Let's just say better safe than sorry."

Danny led the way through the crowded streets toward the temple. Scale seemed especially busy today, though Danny hadn't spent nearly enough time here to say if this was normal or not. Liana took everything in with wide-eyed amazement.

If you'd put a label on her head which read, *I'm from the country, please take advantage of me,* she wouldn't have been a more obvious mark. The more he saw of her innocence, the better asking the priests to look after her sounded.

It didn't take them terribly long to reach the temple. Danny pushed through the always unlocked front door and into the entry area. An older priestess in a white robe with a red cross on the chest sat behind a desk with an open book on it. The layout matched every other temple he'd visited exactly, a fact that did wonders to ease his worries.

"Welcome," the priestess said. "What troubles you today?"

"I've got a bit of a problem, Sister," Danny said. "And the Goddess's temple is the only one I trust to help us."

Her face lit up when she smiled. "We are honored by your trust. Please, tell me what we can do for you."

Danny laid out everything that had happened, editing out the unimportant bits. "Anyway, Liana needs somewhere safe to stay while I see about sorting things out in the forest. I remembered the other temples I visited had these little rooms for guests in need. I was hoping you did as well and that she could stay in one until I know it's safe."

"You did the right thing, bringing her here," the priestess said, her voice warm with sympathy. "We have two rooms free and she can assist in the infirmary to cover the cost of food."

Danny turned to Liana, who looked a bit like a rabbit confronted by a wolf. "What do you think? You'll be safer here than with me. I'm heading back to the forest at first light."

"The Goddess watches over all those who seek shelter under her roof," the priestess added.

"Okay, I'll stay here," Liana said. "I don't know how much help I'll be, but I promise to do my best."

Danny gave her shoulder a squeeze. "That's the spirit. Once I sort this business out, I'll be back to check on you."

She spun around and hugged him. "Thank you for everything."

When she finally let go, he offered a smile. "You're perfectly welcome. Take care of yourself."

With that he turned and walked back out into the afternoon light. Time to test his theory about those drake scales.

No one troubled him on his walk and soon he pushed through the door into the Adventurers' Guild's common room. Only two groups shared the common room and Danny didn't recognize either of them. He hoped that team he rescued made it back okay.

Erin stood at the counter and he made straight for her. She offered a warm and welcoming smile. "Glad you made it back in one piece. I had my doubts when you went in alone. Did you have any luck?"

"A bit." Danny dug three of the scales out and placed them on the counter. "What can I get for these?"

The scales shimmered iridescent green under the lantern light. "I'm pretty sure they're from a lesser earth drake."

Erin nodded and said, "The standard price is two gold pieces. Sound good?"

Danny nodded. "Works for me, thanks."

As she counted the coins, Danny asked, "Did a group called the Glorious Raiders make it back safe?"

"Yeah, about a week ago. They kept talking about the adventurer who drove off a lesser mud drake and saved their lives. You made some new friends."

"Just dumb luck I was in the right place at the right time." He pocketed the coins. "Still, I'm glad they made it back. What about Evard's Blade?"

Erin shook her head. "No clue."

They were probably still in the forest. If they ran into trouble, Danny could do nothing about it. He offered a silent prayer that no one else had the ill luck to encounter a drake.

"You going back out?" Erin asked.

"First thing in the morning. Due to certain circumstances I was forced to return sooner than I planned. Hopefully I can pick up where I left off. Take care."

She laughed. "I should be saying that to you. Good luck."

"I'll take all I can get." He headed for the door. Now to see what the Wizards' Guild would pay for his find.

A five-minute walk brought him to the guild's locked door. Danny knocked and a minute later Howard opened the door dressed in his familiar crimson robe. "This is a surprise. I assumed you'd still be exploring the forest."

"Some stuff happened and I had to return early. Mind if I come in?"

Howard moved aside and Danny walked to the counter that blocked access to the rest of the building. Howard ducked behind it and asked, "Need to look something up in the library?"

"Nope." Danny placed the second trio of drake scales on the counter. "You said the Wizards' Guild will buy direct. What will you give me for these?"

Howard passed a glowing hand over them. "Very nice. I'll give you ten gold coins each."

Danny stared stupidly for a moment. Ten gold? Each? That was five times what the Adventurers' Guild offered. "Are you kidding me?"

"No, that's the going rate. Why?"

"Why? Because the Adventurers' Guild only pays two coins each. If they're selling them to you, that's a bit cheap given who goes into the forest to risk their lives finding them."

Howard held up his hands. "Hey, don't yell at me. I don't set either price. My job is to confirm the authenticity of the specimens and pay the agreed amount. Anything else is out of my hands."

"I'm not mad at you, I'm mad at the situation." He forced himself to relax. "What would you give me for the carcass those scales were attached to?"

Howard laughed then slowly fell silent as Danny stared at him. "You are joking, right?"

"Hell no. Come here." When Howard had joined him, Danny opened his storage. "Take a look. It's reasonably intact too."

Howard stuck his head into the magical space and immediately jerked it back out. "Wait here. The guild master needs to see this."

He rushed through a doorway, robes flapping behind him. Danny closed his storage and leaned against the wall, idly sending one of the gold coins from the guild dancing across his knuckles. Greedy pricks. You'd think a little generosity with the people risking their necks to bring the items back from the forest would be the end of them.

It was ridiculous! But as with many of the problems Danny ran into, he doubted whether he either needed to or should poke his nose into the matter. He had a mission and it didn't include righting all the wrongs of the world.

Two sets of footsteps heralded Howard's return with the guild master. Danny straightened and pocketed his coin.

A scowl crinkled the new man's already wrinkled face even further. He had to be fifty plus at least. A neatly trimmed gray beard covered his chin and cheeks and he wore the same crimson robe as Howard.

The guild master's piercing blue eyes bore into Danny. "What's this nonsense about an intact drake carcass?"

"Ronin, this is Guild Master Feral," Howard said.

Danny nodded and opened his storage. "See for yourself."

"A pocket dimension, and a big one," Feral said. "Impressive. You must have considerable magical potential."

"I do okay. So, are you interested?"

Feral stuck his head inside the white disk. A few seconds later he pulled back. "It's real. Did you kill it or find it?"

Danny didn't care much for Feral's attitude. "Does it matter? Either you're interested in buying it or you're not. There's no way I'm letting Mugg steal eighty percent of my profit."

"You're not the easily intimidated sort I see." A faint quirk twisted Feral's lip upwards. "Of course we want to buy it, but the scales alone are worth thousands of gold coins. The organs, bones, and flesh are worth even more. If I gave you every coin we had in the guild, it wouldn't cover ten percent of the drake's value."

"That's a problem," Danny said. "How do you propose we handle this?"

"I'll pay you ten thousand in gold and twenty-five thousand in gems. I'll also give you a scroll with what you're owed noted in a special magical ink. You can use that at any Wizards' Guild to claim wealth or services."

Danny kept his expression blank, but inside his jaw hit the floor. The hard currency alone would ensure he never needed to worry about money again, to say nothing about the credit scroll.

"Deal. How long do you need to gather my payment?"

"Fifteen minutes. The coin and gems are in the treasury. Writing the scroll is a job of minutes."

"Perfect. Where do you want me to put the drake?"

"The basement. Howard, show Ronin to the processing room. You can leave it right on the floor. None of our tables are close to big enough."

Danny nodded. "As soon as I see the payment, it's all yours. If I should acquire another carcass, would you like me to bring it here?"

Feral's expression grew pained. "Not right away. This find will make us wealthy beyond imagining, but not quickly. I'll need at least a year before I can consider such a purchase."

"Fair enough. Pleasure doing business with you."

"Likewise," Feral said before marching back the way he'd come.

When he was gone Howard said, "I don't suppose I could get a loan?"

Danny smiled. "No, I don't suppose you could."

CHAPTER 9

The flickering glow of a lone candle cast long shadows across the empty common room of the Adventurers' Guild. Guild Master Mugg slumped in his chair, a half-empty cup of ale clutched in his meaty hand. He glowered at nothing and everything. He'd hoped a drink might improve his foul mood, but so far it had only soured his stomach.

Damned useless adventurers. The drake parts and herbs they brought in this month scarcely covered expenses. Mugg's treasury grew emptier by the day. He took another swig and slammed the cup down. Something had to be done.

Exactly what, he had yet to decide.

How could he motivate his members to delve deeper into the forest? Just setting foot under those dark limbs brought high risks. Mugg had made his share of trips during his youth. He wasn't some coward who hid in the city and only worked at headquarters. He'd done his time in the field.

He touched the scar running along the side of his head. This post hadn't come without a price.

His hand reached halfway to the bottle when someone pounded on the door, jolting him from his grim thoughts.

Mugg rose with a growl, knocking over his chair in the process. Who the hell would stop by at this hour? The guild closed hours ago and generally no one would be present. He only came here because he preferred drinking at the guild to the government building.

He stalked across the room, heavy boots thumping on the worn floorboards. Jerking the door open with unnecessary force, he found himself face to face with Feral, his fellow guild master. Unsettlingly bright blue eyes focused on Mugg. Something about the wizard always gave him the creeps.

"Evening, Mugg," Feral said.

"Feral." Mugg grimaced. "What brings you to my door in the dead of night?"

"We need to talk about some things best not overheard by the wrong people."

Mugg didn't like the sound of that one bit. If it got the arrogant wizard out of his precious guild at this hour, it had to be serious.

"Yeah, well, come in then." He stepped aside to allow the wizard to pass.

As soon as Feral cleared the threshold, Mugg slammed the door shut, led the way over to his table, and pointed at the chair opposite his seat. Feral settled in, carefully arranging his crimson robe as he did. Mugg picked his chair off the floor and dropped into it.

He snatched up the bottle of ale and poured the rest into his cup. "You wanted the meeting. Let's hear it."

Feral cleared his throat. "One of your adventurers, a man named Ronin, brought me an intact lesser earth drake carcass today."

Mugg slammed his fist on the table, sending droplets of ale flying. "He did what?! Why the hell is one of *my* adventurers selling directly to *you*?"

The wizard raised an eyebrow. "Because he's aware of how badly you've been taking advantage of *your* adventurers. He was quite vocal about making sure you didn't receive a single coin out of the deal. Ronin's a member of the Wizards' Guild as well, so he's within his rights to sell to me if he chooses."

"Within his rights?" Mugg snarled, leaning forward so his face was inches from Feral's. "What he has the right to do and what's bloody acceptable are very different things!"

His mind raced, trying to calculate how much coin he'd lost on this one transaction. Just thinking about it made his sour stomach all the worse.

"And why didn't you refuse to buy the damn thing?" Mugg jabbed an accusatory finger at Feral. "You know perfectly well those parts rightfully belonged to me!"

Feral bristled, drawing himself up to his full height. "They only belong to you in your arrogant imagination. There's no way I'd pass up such a fantastic opportunity. I can't remember the last time a complete carcass came up for sale. I brought you this news out of respect for our ongoing business relationship. I owe you nothing. This is a courtesy."

Mugg let out a low growl, fingers tightening around his cup until his knuckles turned white and the pewter deformed. The drake would have fetched a fine price, if only he'd gotten his hands on it. Now all that coin was lining Ronin's pockets instead of his own. Damned adventurers, always looking out for themselves. Where was their loyalty?

"I'll be on my way." Feral stood and turned toward the door.

"You'd best think twice before buying directly from my adventurers again." Mugg glared up at him.

To his shock, Feral let out a sharp bark of laughter. "Is that so? Well then, I might just have to rethink the rates I've been giving you for your products." His cold eyes glittered like sapphires in the candlelight. "If that doesn't suit you, feel free to sell them elsewhere. If you can find anyone else who'll take them."

With that parting shot, the wizard turned on his heel and stalked out. The door banged shut, leaving Mugg alone to seethe in impotent rage. Damn the wizard and his miserable guild. Only the wizards knew how to make use of drake parts. He might get something for his herbs from the healers but it would pale in comparison to what the wizards paid.

Damn Feral. Damn Ronin. Damn the whole lot of them! He'd make them pay for this insult.

Mugg started to pour himself a third drink, hands shaking with both anger and drunkenness, only to find the bottle empty. He threw it at the back wall where it shattered, sending glass flying and the dregs dripping to the floor.

His mind raced as he considered his options. Ronin needed killing before he spread word of how bad a deal Mugg offered his members. If the other adventurers found out they could bypass him, he'd be finished. He'd have to find some other way to fund his operations. The prospect didn't appeal to him.

Claiming all the traitorous bastard's lovely gold, on the other hand, appealed to him a great deal.

A slow, cruel smile spread across Mugg's scarred face as a plan took shape. He'd send his enforcers to jump Ronin on the road back to the forest. His best alpha elite adventurers ought to be more than a match for a lone adventurer, even a skilled one. No one would give his disappearance a second thought. People died in the forest all the time. One more wouldn't make a difference.

Mugg chuckled to himself, already counting Ronin's coin. He'd take a nice cut for his trouble, of course, but the rest he'd divide amongst his men as a reward for their loyal service. They'd appreciate that. Keeping the muscle happy always took priority.

This time tomorrow he'd be stacking gold coins, the potential thorn in his side neatly plucked. Mugg could hardly wait.

CHAPTER 10

The dirt road stretched out before Calum. He hated leaving the forest. Open and exposed on the plains and low hills, enemies could see you coming for miles. He vastly preferred the shadows to the glaring sun. Though annoying as the landscape might be, it hardly compared with his irritation at having to stoop to traveling on a human road to a human city. He felt little better than the adventurers who infested his forest.

He'd just have to bear it for a little bit longer. Once he recovered Liana and, heaven willing, completed the ritual, nothing would ever trouble him again. Having to qualify his potential success left him angrier, but Calum refused to lie to himself. Liana's life energy should be enough, but until he added it to the matrix, he wouldn't know for sure.

He crested a rise and at the base of the hill found a small group of men dressed in mail and armed with a variety of weapons lounging in the middle of the road. One of them had to be a wizard based on the ethereal glow around his body.

Calum's lip curled in distaste. More filthy humans. He quickened his pace. The sooner he put the group behind him, the happier he'd be.

But today was not his day. As he approached, the men stepped into his path, barring the way.

"You Ronin?" asked a grizzled human with a jagged scar bisecting one cheek. He had one hand on the hilt of his sword as he stood in the center of the road. He glared at Calum with narrow, squinting eyes.

Calum glared back at the man, his annoyance flaring into anger. How dare these humans impede him! He had no idea who Ronin was, nor did he care. He only knew that he would not tolerate this delay a moment longer.

"Stand aside if you want to keep breathing," Calum said.

The men shifted, closing in on him, hands tightening on weapons. One, a weaselly looking man with dark, beady eyes said, "Ronin's supposed to be comin' from the city. This guy's comin' from the forest."

The leader snorted. "There's only one adventurer crazy enough to travel these parts alone. This has to be him."

The others nodded, seeming persuaded by this sage wisdom. Calum looked on in bafflement. Why did these imbeciles feel the need to discuss this in front of him? But then, attempting to apply logic to the actions of humans was an exercise in futility.

The thought had barely formed when the scarred human said, "Kill him!"

The others roared and drew their weapons. The wizard gathered ether and began to form a spell.

Calum reacted instantly. Ether gathered around his hands and he hurled crackling bolts of lightning in every direction.

It struck each of the men, arcing between them. They

screamed and twitched and thrashed as his magic burned their lives away.

Before he could finish them, the wizard cut off the ether, ending his spell.

The leader grimaced and pushed off the ground, steam rising from his singed body. His companions struggled, slower to regain their feet.

The wizard's effort impressed him. He wouldn't have thought a human capable of interrupting his magic. Not that it would save them.

A focused lance of ether shot out from the tip of his finger and hammered into the wizard's skull, blowing it to pieces.

Calum spun to avoid an overhead slash from the lead human's sword. As he passed, Calum tapped the man's head, releasing a pulse of concussive force that blew his head to pulp.

Streams of blue flames streaked out, burning through the survivors in seconds.

Then silence returned and he found himself alone again. Corpses littered the road and the reek of scorched meat filled the air. Calum stood amidst the carnage, not even breathing hard. Pathetic creatures.

Shaking his head in disgust, he stepped over the bodies and continued on his way.

Miles passed without further trouble until he sensed another life force approaching, another human. And it was coming quickly.

A moment later he spotted a lone figure rushing down the road toward him. The human ran flat out, raising a cloud of dust behind him. He swerved to avoid Calum at the last second, not even sparing him a glance as he hurtled past.

Calum's eyes narrowed. The runner's garb and gear marked him as an adventurer. An adventurer heading away from Scale City, not toward it. Interesting. Perhaps this was the mysterious Ronin his attackers sought.

In any case it didn't matter one way or the other to him. Calum put the encounter out of his mind and pressed on.

Hours later, the walls of Scale finally came into view. How long had it been since Calum last visited? He didn't remember, but years certainly and possibly decades. He'd done his best to bury the memories of his last visit down deep.

Calum's lip curled in disdain. He loathed everything about human cities, the noise, the filth, the press of bodies, it all disgusted him. But Liana had to be here somewhere and he would find her. No one stole from him and escaped. He refused to accept it.

A modest group of six human soldiers stood around the gate looking bored. Calling such lax individuals guards was overly generous. They did make a credible effort to straighten as he approached.

One of the men asked, "Do you have a guild card?"

Calum pulled out his Wizards' Guild card and showed it to the human. "Will this suffice?"

"Yup, that's fine. Welcome back to Scale."

Calum swept past, putting his card away as he did. He'd joined on a whim during his last visit. Looked like the effort had been worthwhile. Those weaklings had no hope of stopping him if they wished to, but avoiding a ruckus served

Calum's interests better. He needed information, not pointless combat.

He'd try the Wizards' Guild first. Mostly because, as a member, he assumed they'd be the ones most likely to speak with him. Hopefully they'd know something useful.

His memory of the city remained adequate to guide him to the three-story stone building. A hard knock on the door echoed through the quiet street. After a long moment, it creaked open, revealing a thin, unsmiling man in red robes. "We're not open to the public."

He moved to shut the door. Calum's hand shot out, catching it before it closed. He gritted his teeth, forcing himself to remain calm. "I'm not the public." He held up his guild card for inspection.

The human peered at the card then he sighed and stepped back, allowing Calum to enter. "Sorry, I didn't recognize you. You must be from outside the city."

Calum smiled in amusement at the irony of his words. "Indeed, I haven't been to Scale in some time. However, circumstances have made it necessary."

"Follow me, Mr…"

"Calum."

"Mr. Calum. I'm Howard, the newest employee of the guild. Which is how I got stuck answering the door." The human muttered that last sentence under his breath, but Calum's sharp hearing caught the words.

They reached the entry area and Howard ducked behind the counter. "So, how can the guild be of assistance?"

"I'm looking for someone. A young woman who may have recently arrived in the city. Her name is Liana."

Howard offered a wry smile and shook his head. "I'm afraid I don't see many young women in my line of work, more's the pity. If any have recently arrived, I know nothing about it."

Calum forced himself to take a calming breath. He knew it wasn't going to be that simple. "Has anything else of interest occurred lately? Anything... unusual?"

Howard hesitated, then shrugged. "I guess it's not a secret. An adventurer brought in a lesser earth drake carcass yesterday. That's pretty rare. The guild master was most excited."

Calum's eyes narrowed. He didn't believe in coincidences. First his servant drake goes missing then one of the same species shows up here? No, whoever brought that carcass to the city had to be the same person who had spirited Liana away from the sacrificial site. He leaned in closer to Howard, his voice low and intent.

"Who sold the carcass to the guild?"

"An adventurer named Ronin." Howard shifted to put a bit more distance between them. "Seemed like a nice guy. He's a member of our guild as well."

Calum's thoughts flashed back to the encounter on the road. The adventurers had mistaken him for Ronin. Then he passed the lone traveler coming from the city. Assuming he guessed correctly about the man's identity, it would seem his prey's guardian had left the city. How convenient.

"Was there anything else?" Howard asked.

Calum had been so deep in thought he'd forgotten the human was there. "No. You've been very helpful. Good evening."

He turned on his heel and headed for the door. The Adventurers' Guild would be his next stop. Surely someone there would know where Ronin lived and, more importantly, where he could find Liana.

CHAPTER 11

Danny pounded down the dirt road, kicking up clouds of dust behind him as he ran at a relentless pace. His side trip had cost him most of two weeks and while nothing said he needed to find the ether pool quickly, he also didn't dare screw around too much. He had nineteen left and a huge continent to traverse.

At least he found a safe place for Liana back in Scale City and his storage now bulged with supplies. He should be able to finish his mission without further distractions.

Well, mostly without distractions. A nagging question remained in the back of his mind. How would he handle the Master of Drakes? Danny had no idea where the sorcerer made his lair within the sprawling wilderness. The odds of simply stumbling across it were slim at best. Unlike the ether pool, Danny didn't know where to begin looking for his base.

He gave a little shake of his head. No point worrying about it. Danny would deal with him when he had to. For now, he needed to focus on things within his control.

A dozen miles from the city, Danny sensed a lone life force on the road ahead of him. It reminded him of Lyra, but closer to a human. Were there any elf-bloods in the Adventurers' Guild? He didn't know but couldn't imagine someone out here being anything other than an adventurer.

Moments later, he spotted a solitary figure walking up ahead. The elf-blood wore a dark green cloak with the hood up. Danny didn't pause to chat. Whoever he was and whatever his business, it had nothing to do with Danny. He caught a glimpse of hard, angry eyes looking his way as he passed.

Half a mile later he'd put the wanderer out of his thoughts. The forest drew ever closer and he needed to concentrate.

Or so he intended. A few miles further on he spotted five bodies littering the road. He skidded to a halt and surveyed the grim scene. The dead men had been ill-used by something. Two of their heads had been destroyed and horrific burns covered the rest of them. In his old world, Danny would've assumed a road-side bomb had gone off.

Here his assumption switched from a bomb to magic. He took a closer look at their gear. The weapons looked well used as did the armor. Whoever they were, they'd been at their trade for a while. A group this small and in this place had to be adventurers, but Danny didn't recognize any of them. He blew out a sigh of relief. The few groups he knew, he liked well enough not to want to see them dead.

Danny might not have been the greatest hunter in the world, but he had sufficient skill to tell no tracks led to or away from the road. Nothing indicated a drake did this. In fact, Danny couldn't remember ever hearing about an attack outside the forest. But if a drake didn't attack the group, what did? Nothing he saw made any sense. At least not with the information he had on hand.

In any case, leaving them here to rot in the sun didn't sit right with Danny. As fellow adventurers, he owed them a proper burial. He'd moved his share of bodies over the years and this wasn't even the worst-mangled bunch. The lack of body bags made the task nastier than usual, but he managed all the same. The process took about ten minutes and once he had them safely in his storage Danny got back on the road.

He ran until he spotted the adventurers' campsite near dusk. Two fires burned a fair distance from each other. Hopefully someone could identify the bodies he found.

As he approached, Danny recognized Evard's Blade. Though he didn't consider them friends, he'd had enough interactions with the group to be relieved that they made it out of the forest in one piece.

"Well, look who it is." Brand stood, a cocky sneer on his face. "You didn't last long in the forest despite all your big talk about working alone. You already had to run back to the city. Pitiful."

Danny rolled his eyes and ignored the idiot's taunting. Flattening him wasn't worth the minute amount of effort it would take.

"How many times do I have to tell you to stow that kind of talk, Brand?" Evard said. "You about pissed yourself the first time a bush rustled."

Despite the poor light, Danny noticed Brand's cheeks color as his companions laughed, and he quickly sat back down.

"Don't mind him," Evard said. "We all heard what you did

for the Glorious Raiders. Damn lucky for them you were around."

"I was just in the right place at the right time. Anyone would've done the same thing." Danny lowered his voice. "Can we talk a minute, privately? It's important."

"Sure, lad. Come on." They moved a ways from the campfire, out of earshot of the others. "What's on your mind?"

"I found some bodies on the road," he said. "A whole group of adventurers, and not rookies, judging by their gear. Burned and crushed to death."

Evard's eyes widened. "Heaven's mercy. Where? How many?"

"Half a day's run west of here. As for the bodies, you can see for yourself." Danny opened his storage and motioned for Evard to take a look.

The older man stuck his head into the opening and immediately jerked it back. "I know them, Mugg's skull kickers. They were alpha elite adventurers. There's no way something took them by surprise, which means they fought something stronger than them. Not an encouraging thought."

"No, it isn't. I saw no tracks or other indications a drake attacked them. Though what we know about all of their abilities isn't exactly comprehensive." Danny hesitated then added, "I thought it might be demons, but I sensed no corruption, so I think we're in the clear there."

"Thank Branik for small favors." Evard made the sign of the inverted sword over his chest.

Danny seconded that. "I'm not sure what to do with the bodies. Do they have families in the city?"

"This lot? I doubt it. We'll bury them here. There's a graveyard for fallen adventurers at the edge of the campsite.

We're headed back to the city in the morning to sell our take. We'll let Mugg know what happened to his people." Evard shook his head. "He's not going to be pleased."

Given what he knew about the guild master, Danny didn't really care how displeasing he found the news. "Best be extra careful on your way home. If whatever did this is still around, it might target your team next."

"We will be, rest assured. But the same goes for you in the forest. I've got no interest in digging your grave."

Danny appreciated the sentiment, but if anything happened to him, his body would end up swallowed by the forest with no one the wiser.

With that pleasant thought in mind, he followed Evard to the little graveyard on the edge of the campsite. They had digging to do and then Danny needed some sleep. He had a long way to go and wanted to get an early start in the morning.

CHAPTER 12

After a night spent resting in the dubious comfort of a human-run inn, Calum finally arrived at the Adventurers' Guild. His original plan had been to visit immediately after leaving the Wizards' Guild the night before but when he arrived, he found the door locked tight and not a soul in sight, a modest but still irksome delay.

He stalked through the door and into the common room. Glancing around, he did his best to keep any disgust from showing. Rowdy, stinking humans, men and women both, gathered around rough-hewn tables, boasting of their plans to explore the Forest of Drakes. His forest! As if stealing the many herbs growing there, whatever drake scales they stumbled across, or smaller beasts they slew was no problem.

The stench of stale ale, sweat, and leather armor nearly made him gag. This place was so much worse than the Wizards' Guild. It felt like someone had taken every bad thing about humanity, compacted it, and shoved it into one building. It might well be the worst place he'd ever visited.

Steeling himself, Calum made his way to the counter

where two clerks stood. On the right, a man with a patchy beard scratched notes in a ledger and on the left, a buxom brunette in a low-cut green tunic smiled brightly at customers. Calum approached the woman.

"Welcome! Are you a member of the guild?" Her perky voice grated on his ears but he somehow kept expression bland. At least he hoped he did.

"No," Calum said. "I'm with the Wizards' Guild. They suggested I inquire here about the whereabouts of an adventurer named Ronin. I need to speak with him."

The clerk tapped a finger on her front tooth as she mused. "Ronin's a new arrival in Scale. I'm afraid I don't know much about him."

"I see." Calum kept his temper firmly under control. "Do you know where he lives? An address where I might find him?"

"Oh, I'm fairly certain he hasn't purchased a home. Most adventurers just rent rooms at the local inns when they're in town between expeditions." Erin shrugged. "But I don't know which inn he's staying at right now. Sorry I can't be of more help."

Calum exhaled slowly through his nose. Murdering the useless girl would only slow his progress further. Finding the warrior who had stolen his sacrifice would prove more difficult than he hoped, but no matter.

"Very well. My thanks for your time," he said with icy politeness before turning toward the exit.

A burly man with a jagged scar running up his scalp intercepted Calum midstride. "Couldn't help overhearing. What's your business with Ronin?"

The human's dark eyes bore into Calum with obvious suspicion.

Calum didn't care. He'd reached the end of his patience. "I merely wish to speak with him about a young woman who recently went missing from my village. I believe he may know something about her."

"You saying Ronin kidnapped her or something?" The man crossed his arms.

"I make no accusations, but I do need to find her and I think he's my best chance to do so."

"Well, you're out of luck. Ronin headed for the Forest of Drakes at first light yesterday."

Calum's lips thinned. The man he'd met on the road likely was Ronin, as he'd thought. "I see. Well then, you have my gratitude for the information." He inclined his head slightly and made to leave.

"A word of advice," the man said. "Forget about following Ronin. That forest's a death trap. He made it out once, not likely he'll do so a second time."

Calum found no fault in the human's understanding of his home's danger. Should Ronin die, Calum would shed no tears, but it would make finding Liana all the harder. On the plus side, she had at least been separated from her rescuer. When he found her, he'd have no trouble bringing her back.

Outside the guild he took a deep breath and grimaced at whatever sizzled over the fire at a nearby food stall. Some of the things humans ate didn't bear close scrutiny. The fact that so many of them survived as long as they did was a small miracle. Or perhaps more accurately, a curse from one of the nine hells.

Maybe the guards at the city gate had seen something useful. A dubious prospect, but best not to leave any stone unturned. Calum set out toward the gate. The city only had one, so if they hadn't seen Liana, he didn't know who might've.

When he arrived, he found the same louts who let him in the evening he arrived. If they remembered him, they gave no sign.

"Help you with something?" one of the guards asked.

"I'm looking for someone, a young woman from my village. She would've arrived in the last few days in the company of an adventurer."

The guards looked at each other then the spokesman asked, "How much might this information be worth to you?"

Of course they wanted gold. These miserable creatures thought about little else. He reached into a hidden pocket and pulled out a pouch which jingled when he shook it. "If you know something useful, you'll be rewarded."

"You heard him," the spokesman said. "Anyone remember anything like that?"

"I do!" a younger-looking human said. "I don't usually pay much attention but she was a knockout. Weirdest thing too, she had cloth strips wrapped around her feet instead of shoes."

Since she'd been staked out naked for sacrifice, that made sense.

"And did you see where she went after entering the city?" Calum asked. Confirming her presence in the city came as a relief, but he needed more.

The guard scratched his chin. "No, sorry. Couldn't leave my post no matter how pretty she was. I need this job."

Calum exhaled slowly. Another dead end. He tossed them the pouch, turned, and strode away without another word. It seemed he needed to use his magic to find her. Searching a city this size would leave him drained for hours, which was why he'd done his best to find her in other ways.

He hurried back to his rented room. The inn he'd selected at least had clean rooms and edible food. Considering where he found himself, that exceeded his expectations.

When he finally arrived and closed the door behind him, Calum settled cross-legged on the rough blanket covering his cot. He closed his eyes and called the ether. He shaped it into magical eyes and sent his sight soaring over the city.

Passing through walls and peering into windows, he searched for any sign of the girl. One by one, he eliminated the possibilities until only the temples and Wizards' Guild remained. Since he felt confident Ronin didn't leave her at the guild, that meant she must be taking shelter at one of the temples. Unfortunately for him, they had wards to stop magical spying.

He'd have to complete his search up close and personal.

Calum spent the rest of the morning regaining the strength he'd spent on his magical search, then set out to visit the temples. The easiest way to approach them would be as a worried family member, her brother perhaps. Despite his many centuries of life, Calum easily passed for a man in his twenties.

The walk to the city center didn't take overly long and soon Calum found himself standing across the street from Branik's temple. He could hardly imagine a less inviting design for a temple than this grim stone fortress. At the entrance, two guards in armor stood at full alert as if expecting an attack at any moment.

The guards shifted to block his approach. "Do you have business here?" one of them asked.

Calum plastered on a distraught expression. "Please, I'm looking for my sister. She disappeared from our village and I'm worried she might have been taken by a man named Ronin. Has a young woman been brought here recently?"

The guards exchanged a look and the speaker said, "No young ladies have been brought to the temple, sir."

"I see. Thank you, gentlemen, very much." Calum hurried on. One down and two to go. The city's lack of a robust collection of temples would make his life easier today.

Adonael's came next. He walked right through the unlocked door. Inside, a skinny little human wearing a white robe with the halo symbol on his breast busied himself cleaning the pews. He looked up as Calum approached, his face pale and eyes wide. He relaxed as soon as he saw Calum.

"Can I help you?" the priest asked.

He repeated his story and at the mention of Ronin's name, the priest looked nearly ready to faint.

"You know Ronin?" the priest asked, voice trembling.

Calum shook his head. "Not personally. But as I said I fear he kidnapped my sister. Why, has he wronged you as well?"

The priest licked his lips. "Not me, Adonael. Ronin is an enemy of our faith."

"I see." A slow smile spread across Calum's face. He might be able to use this idiot. "Can you help me find my sister?"

"Ronin is too powerful to take her back if he really doesn't wish to give her up."

"He's not with her and she's nowhere I can find in the city. I asked at Branik's temple and they hadn't seen her."

"I haven't either. She might be at the Goddess's temple.

They have rooms for people in trouble." The priest frowned. "If he kidnapped her, why would he leave her at a temple liable to protect her and then leave?"

"Who can say? Perhaps I have the situation all wrong. I haven't spoken to either of them. My wish is to find my sister safe and sound. Nothing else matters."

"If she's at the Goddess's temple, you will find her well, that much I can assure you. And should you find and kill Ronin, bring proof to me and you will be well rewarded."

"Thank you for your help." So saying, Calum strode from the temple. She had to be in the Goddess's temple, and if she was, one way or another he'd have her.

Only a few dozen strides separated the temples and soon enough he walked through the entrance. A priestess in a white robe greeted him with a warm smile. "How may I assist you?"

Calum forced a strained smile. "I'm looking for my sister, Liana. I have reason to believe she may have been brought here against her will by a man named Ronin."

The priestess's brow furrowed. "A young woman was indeed brought to us recently, seeking sanctuary. She's under our protection now."

"I am her brother," Calum said. "And I've come to bring her home."

"Wait here. I'll speak with her and she can decide if she wishes to go with you or not." The priestess ducked out of sight down a nearby hall.

Calum debated following her but decided to stick with his worried-brother routine.

Five minutes later the priestess returned, alone, her expression grim. "Liana says she has no brother. I must ask you to leave. Now."

Rage, far too long suppressed, ignited in Calum's veins. How dare this human defy him? He gathered ether until the air fairly crackled. "You will turn her over to me this instant," he snarled. "Or I will take her by force."

A blinding golden aura flared to life around the priestess. Calum flew backwards and slammed into the wall. "Liana is under the Goddess's protection, as am I, as is this place. Be gone, unless you wish to face the wrath of an archangel."

He sensed more priests coming from deeper in the temple. He couldn't win this battle, not now anyway.

Dazed, Calum staggered to his feet and fled. He hurried for the gate, eager to leave the wretched city behind. And even more eager to gather a force of drakes to burn it to the ground.

CHAPTER 13

Danny raced through the shadowy depths of the Forest of Drakes. As the days and hours went by he got more and more confident in his stealth field's protection, and the more confident he got, the faster he ran. Thanks to that increase in speed, he was finally approaching the center of the forest. This deep in, the dense canopy blocked out most of the sunlight, creating an oppressive, chill gloom.

Though he often sensed their life forces in the distance, Danny hadn't encountered a single drake. Once or twice, he glimpsed the dark shapes of greater drakes soaring by, but they acted oblivious to his presence. Whether they really couldn't sense him or they just considered him unthreatening, he neither knew nor cared. As long as they left him alone, he'd happily return the favor.

He paused and checked the ether. Tiny streaks ran through it. The ether pool had to be close and thank heaven for that. If he never had to run through another forest, he'd consider himself fortunate. Maybe he'd get lucky and finish with this one today.

Danny got moving again and soon the trees started to thin, then they ended. He froze at the edge of a wide clearing, his jaw dropping at the sight before him. In the center of the clearing, a towering black stone castle stabbed into the sky. No protective walls surrounded the main keep. Whether the lack of protection indicated confidence or arrogance Danny had no idea.

No way did the elf-bloods leave an ether pool without serious guardians. Best to have a look around before he got too close.

As he circled the perimeter, Danny studied the walls. The castle looked to be in pristine condition. No cracks marred the faces of the stones and no moss or lichen clung to the mortar. The perfectly symmetrical arrow slits looked as flawless as the day the mason built them. It sure didn't look at all like the elf-blood buildings he'd seen before. Where was the smooth steel?

He took a deep breath to steady his nerves. One way to find out for sure.

Danny approached the castle gate, every sense alert for danger. In the ether, the faint glowing streams grew thicker by the moment, confirming the ether pool's presence in the process. He scanned the area for any sign of wards or other protective enchantments but saw nothing.

The whole setup struck him as weird, and he didn't trust it for a second. After his brutal battle against the digger constructs in the crystal mine, he knew without a doubt that something or someone was going to appear and try to stop him from reaching the pool and destroying it. A castle had to have soldiers and knights, right? Maybe there'd be construct versions of them.

He'd covered half the distance to the gate when it slowly creaked open. It sounded like a door in a horror movie right before the monster sprang out. Danny was ready to grab the ethersword at the first sign of danger, but he didn't want to do anything aggressive. Avoiding a fight would be ideal.

A figure emerged from the shadows of the entryway, but it wasn't a monster. Instead, a strikingly beautiful woman with long, dark-red hair and a body that put Princess Claudette to shame strode toward him. Her dress appeared to be woven from the very fabric of the night, including sparkles that might be stars. As she moved closer, Danny sensed a powerful magical aura surrounding her. He'd never encountered anything like it.

She stopped ten yards from the gate and made no hostile moves. Cautiously, Danny continued his approach, careful to keep his movements slow and non-threatening. If she didn't start anything he certainly wouldn't.

When he was just a few feet away, the woman spoke, her melodic voice as beautiful as the rest of her. "Who are you, and what business do you have here?"

Danny met her gaze. "My name is Ronin and I've come to destroy the ether pool beneath this castle."

The woman's dark eyes narrowed. "I am Marlina and I'm afraid I cannot allow you to enter."

Danny frowned. "That's going to be a problem. There are eighteen more of these things and I need to destroy them, or at least enough of them to sever the connection between Earth and Valindor."

Marlina's brow furrowed. "You are remarkably well informed for a human. I doubt many people are even aware of the pools, much less their purpose. But you said eighteen —there should be nineteen plus this one."

"There were, I already destroyed the one under the Crystal Mist Mountains. This was my next stop."

"Would you mind telling me your story? Clearly you're different from the usual intruder who approaches the castle."

Danny didn't mind telling her, but she'd tickled his curiosity. "Do you get many intruders? Just traveling through a drake-filled forest would be impossible for most people."

"I've had a few over the last fifteen hundred years. I think you're the sixth."

Danny certainly wouldn't call that too many. He gave a little shake of his head and launched into his story. He didn't cover every detail, that would take too long, but he did hit the highlights. "Anyway, I don't want anyone else from my world to end up summoned here, thus the ether pools must go."

When Danny finished his story, Marlina sighed. "A remarkable tale. I wish I could let you pass, but the magic that binds me to this place prevents me from doing so."

"Wait." How could he have been so blind? She wasn't an elf-blood or a demon, which meant that to live this long she had to be something else. "You're a transformed greater drake, aren't you?"

Her eyes widened. "How did you know?"

"Considering your magical aura, how long you've been here, that you referred to me as a human, and where we are, it was a logical guess," Danny said. "Listen, I don't want to kill another drake if I can avoid it. Is there any way to break the binding?"

Marlina hesitated. "There is one way, but it's dangerous."

"Danger bothers me less than killing someone who

doesn't deserve it. I've had to do more of that than I like since my summoning."

"Very well. You must destroy the Flute of Controlling Drakes. Its current wielder, while not strong enough to command greater drakes like myself, can still control my lesser cousins."

"The Master of Drakes. I knew he was going to be a problem. While I didn't think he'd be a direct obstacle to destroying the pool, I'm not shocked either."

"You know him?" she asked, surprise clear in her tone.

"Not personally. According to the girl I rescued, Liana, he rules a village of humans and takes a sacrifice every five years. What he might want with a pretty human girl I prefer not to think too hard about."

"I can assure you he doesn't want them for what you're thinking, and he rules five villages, not one," Marlina said. "He's an elf-blood and an arrogant one. He came to this castle once and attempted to bend me to his will. He failed. I can only assume he's collecting life force for a spell. He wants the castle. He thinks it's his birthright since a half-elf built it. If he gathers enough power and combines it with the flute, he might be able to seize control of me."

"I've seen what a greater drake can do. Stopping him just moved way up on my to-do list."

She cocked her head. "When did you see that?"

Danny had skipped over his encounter with Merrok when he told his story. Talking about the corrupted fire drake seemed in bad taste given his audience. "It's not a nice story. Are you sure you want to hear it?"

Marlina nodded.

"It happened when I was in the Five Kingdoms. The cult of Ardent Lilly had captured and corrupted a fire drake.

They sent him to attack a kingdom city. I drove him off then my companions and I hunted him down. It was nearly as tough a battle as the one I fought with the demon king, but in the end, I freed him from the cult's control. Unfortunately, the corruption had spread too far and I couldn't save him. He asked me to end his life before he transformed into something evil. I did as he bid. Not being able to save him is among the biggest of my many disappointments."

Marlina had begun trembling partway through the story. "Do you know the drake's name?"

"Merrok. He was my friend. The first real friend I made in this world, even if it was only for a few minutes. Why?"

"He was my son. Merrok disappeared a decade ago and I never knew where he went or what became of him. He was always diligent about returning to visit me. When he stopped, I knew something bad had happened." Tears ran down her face. "My poor boy."

Before good sense got the better of him, Danny closed the distance between them and hugged her. Marlina stiffened for a second then melted into him. He held her while she cried.

When she finally got herself under control, she moved back. "Thank you for telling me. I felt the truth of your words and the strength of your friendship with my son. I'm glad you were with him at the end. And I'm glad you killed the ones responsible."

"So am I. Do you know where I can find the Master of Drakes?"

"I know he has a home in the forest, but I fear I don't know exactly where."

"That's okay. Liana might know. I'll head back to the city and ask her. I promise to do my best to free you from the binding. Now that I know you're Merrok's mom, I couldn't fight you if I had to."

Pain shadowed her smile. Marlina took a step closer and kissed his cheek. Ether swirled around him when she did. "Take my blessing. No free drake will harm you now. Those compelled by the flute are another matter."

"Why would the other drakes listen to you?"

"Because I am the queen of the forest. I was here before the half-elf and his cursed flute arrived and I will be here until the world ends."

"Wow. I didn't know Merrok was a prince. I'll try to be worthy of your blessing. Until we meet again."

Danny bowed, turned, and ran into the forest. He needed to return as quickly as possible. Finding and defeating the Master of Drakes would not only free Marlina, but the human villages as well.

That was a goal well worth his effort.

CHAPTER 14

Mugg slammed his empty cup on the wooden table. Foam from sloshed ale dripped down the sides. Only a handful of people filled the Adventurers' Guild's common room. Most honest folk had already gone off to work at this hour. But not Mugg. He glowered at nothing in particular, his eyes bleary and unfocused after three big bottles of ale. The last few days, or weeks, or however much time had passed, he'd been hitting the bottle pretty hard and he felt it down to his toes.

Damn Ronin! First the bastard humiliated Mugg by denying him the guild's proper cut of the drake sale, then he went and killed Mugg's best enforcers. Oh, Evard claimed some monster killed them on the road and Ronin just found the bodies, but Mugg knew better. He'd sent the useless idiots to kill the man after all. How had Ronin turned the tables on such experienced adventurers? It should've been impossible, but they died and Ronin lived so he couldn't exactly argue about the facts.

He reached for the half-full bottle to refill his cup. Noon

hadn't arrived yet, but no one had the guts to criticize the guild master. He shot a glare at the clerks who had their heads down as they worked behind the counter. Neither of them paid him the least attention. For some reason that irritated Mugg more than their condemning looks would've. It was like they didn't even consider him worth criticizing.

He had the bottle halfway to his cup, almost ready to pour, when the doors burst open and a city guard hurried in, his face pale and grim beneath his helm. What could've gotten the lazy lout moving so quickly? Mugg needed another problem like he needed a broken leg.

"Mayor! Terrible news!" the guard shouted.

Mugg grimaced at the volume. "I'm standing right in front of you, idiot. Pipe down."

"Sorry, sir. But half a dozen drakes are approaching the city as we speak. We've sealed the gate but what should we do now?"

Mugg stared at the guard, his ale-soaked mind struggling to process what the man just said. Drakes? Approaching his city? That had never happened. Not just in the ten years since he took over, but ever. Drakes didn't gather in groups and they didn't leave the forest. The solitary creatures constantly fought over territory. Why was his whole world unraveling all of a sudden?

His fist clenched, squashing his pewter cup. No. He would not let everything he'd built fall to ruin.

"Show me." Mugg got to his feet and stalked after the guard, his stride steadier than he'd feared it might be.

Outside, the too-bright daylight stabbed his eyes, forcing him to squint against the glare. He didn't let it slow him down, and soon they reached the city wall and started climbing the stairs to the battlements.

What he saw sobered him up in a hurry.

About a quarter mile out, six scaly shapes of varying colors and sizes ran toward the city. Lesser drakes, but he found that a cold comfort. Should they attack, the city wouldn't last ten minutes.

The drakes stopped just out of ballista range. He knew they were supposed to be smart, but he'd assumed that meant animal cunning. Their actions suggested something greater. Something worse for Scale City.

"Sir," the guard said. "Am I crazy or does the biggest one have a rider?"

Mugg squinted harder. Sure enough, a small figure perched atop the lead drake.

A chill ran down his spine. Who in the hells could ride a drake? No wizard he'd ever heard of had strength enough for such a thing. And he had to be controlling the rest of them as well.

This was so bad. What should they do?

"Load the ballistae," Mugg said.

"Already done, sir," one of the artillerists said.

He turned back in time to watch the rider urge his mount forward. Mugg tensed. The rider, a man judging by his frame, dressed in a deep-green cloak and matching trousers, showed no sign of fear.

When he crossed the hundred-yards-out mark, Mugg said, "Fire!"

The ballista thunked and launched its steel-tipped bolt right at them.

The bolt stopped six inches short of impact and dropped to the ground. The drake continued forward as if nothing had happened. At ten yards out the drake stopped and the rider shouted in an amplified voice. "I would speak with your leader."

"You're speaking to him," Mugg shouted back. The wizard's voice sounded vaguely familiar, but his ale-soaked brain refused to place it.

"I'll make this brief," the rider said. "There's a girl named Liana taking refuge in the temple of the Goddess. Hand her over and I and my drakes will leave peacefully. Refuse, and I'll level this city and kill everyone inside. You have one hour to send her out."

So saying, the rider turned his mount around and showed them his back. The sheer contempt of the move made Mugg bristle. He hated the idea of giving in to the arrogant bastard, but he hated the idea of getting eaten by a drake even more. The question was, would the temple agree to hand her over?

Only one way to find out. "Keep watch here. I'm going to the temple."

He hurried down the nearby steps and turned toward the city center. The walk gave him a chance to finish gathering his wits. Even with the ballistae and whatever fighters they could gather, six drakes overmatched them by a lot. They might kill one or two, but in the end, the city would fall.

He reached the temple and pushed through the unlocked door. A priestess stood behind the welcome desk. She smiled and asked, "How may I help you, Mayor Mugg?"

"We have a situation." Mugg gave her a brief explanation. "So if we don't hand Liana over, he'll raze the city to the ground. Where is she? The sooner she's out of the city, the better."

"Liana is under the Goddess's protection. I can't hand her over."

"Would you really trade the entire city to save one girl? How does that serve the greater good?"

Color drained from the priestess's face, but she held firm. "It's not our decision. The Goddess has given Liana Her protection, not us. The request came from one she has touched. What will she think of us, how will she judge us, if we fail?"

"Are you telling me Ronin has been touched by the Goddess?" Mugg didn't believe it. No wonder he couldn't get the best of the man. He had Heaven's blessing.

The priestess nodded, confirming his fear.

"Wait," a soft voice said. He'd been so focused on the priestess he hadn't noticed possibly the most beautiful woman he'd ever seen come in from the infirmary. "I'll go with him. I don't want anyone to die for me."

"You don't have to do this, Liana," the priestess said. "The Goddess will protect you as we promised Ronin."

Liana shook her head, tears glinting in her dark eyes. "I thought I could fight my destiny. But it seems I can't. The Master of Drakes won't let me. When Ronin gets back, thank him for me and tell him I'm sorry I couldn't stay safe the way he wanted."

Some small part of Mugg felt a grudging respect for the girl. She had guts, no question. A bigger part was flooded with relief. Ronin might well kill him when he found out what happened, but Mugg would deal with that possibility later.

"Come on." He took Liana by the elbow. "I don't want to give that lunatic any reason to think we're not going to comply."

Liana meekly let him lead her away. As they hurried

toward the gate, Mugg felt something he hadn't experienced in a long time. Guilt.

Liana winced as Mugg gripped her elbow, practically dragging her through the streets of Scale City. He acted like he feared she might try and run. Not that she didn't want to run, but she'd already tried to escape once and look how that worked out. Fate, for whatever reason, wanted her to feed the great ones.

She flicked a glance at Mugg. His stench, a foul mixture of sweat and rancid breath, nearly made her gag. She'd met many kind and wonderful people since coming here, which made having to deal with someone like him all the worse.

"Keep moving, it's not far now," Mugg said. "You're doing the right thing. A lot of people are going to live thanks to you."

The way he talked made her think he spoke more to himself than to her. Like he was struggling to convince himself he'd made the right choice. Perhaps he wasn't as bad as she thought. Liana of all people appreciated how terrifying the Master of Drakes could be. The only sensible reactions when you met him were fear and desperation.

She almost smiled. Ronin hadn't been afraid of him or the drakes. He'd been so eager to help her, to keep her safe. Her own family happily handed her over, but not him. Liana regretted that she wouldn't be able to see him again.

They approached the city gate, but a heavy steel portcullis barred their path. "Open up!" Mugg shouted to the guards.

The gate clanked slowly out of sight. Liana's heart raced and she feared she might faint. Beyond the walls, the great ones waited. Six of them, with the Master of Drakes seated on the largest. She'd never seen more than one before. This many nearly overwhelmed her.

The moment the portcullis lifted high enough for her to step through, Mugg gave her a little shove. She barely heard him mutter, "Good luck."

The portcullis crashed back down behind her, making it clear changing her mind wasn't an option.

Liana took a deep, shaky breath. This was it. She tried to escape her fate but the world didn't work that way. She should've known. Maybe she did, deep down. But Liana had so wanted to believe in the wonderful dream Ronin had showed her.

But that's all it had been, a dream. Squaring her shoulders, she walked toward the great ones. Her entire body trembled, but she pressed on.

A few yards out, the yellow-scaled great one sent its forked tongue flicking out to taste her scent. Liana froze, certain it meant to devour her on the spot.

"You've caused me a great deal of extra work," a cold voice said from above. "Did you really think you had any hope of escaping?"

Liana looked up into the eyes of the Master of Drakes. She opened her mouth, but no words came out. Her throat constricted with fear, leaving her mute and paralyzed. She stared at him, a mouse cornered by a snake.

The Master gestured and an invisible force grabbed Liana and lifted her off the ground. She let out a yelp as his magic deposited her on the great one behind him.

Magical bonds held her still and in place, lashing her to the great one's rough scales like a piece of luggage. The beast shifted beneath her. The muscle moving beneath its scales felt slimy despite their dryness.

Without another word, the Master wheeled his mount around and all six great ones ran for the forest. Liana tried her best to stay calm. She'd spared the city at least. She took some pride in that. Whatever happened next was out of her hands.

Though she did hope that being devoured wouldn't be too painful.

CHAPTER 15

Danny sprinted down the road toward Scale City. After receiving Marlina's blessing he didn't bother with his stealth field, instead putting all his power into increasing his speed. The sooner he dealt with the Master of Drakes, the better he'd feel. Especially since it would free Merrok's mom from the binding holding her in the castle. He smiled when he thought of her. What were the odds of him running into his friend's mom all the way out here? Insanely small seemed about right. Danny resolved to do his best for her.

Half an hour later the city came into view. He frowned and slowed a fraction. The guards had lowered the portcullis. It hadn't been lowered for as long as Danny had been coming and going. In fact, he'd doubted the mechanism worked. What could've convinced them to drop it now? Whatever happened, it must've been serious.

When he arrived, he found the usual guards on duty, but they stood on the other side of the portcullis, peering out at him through the bars. Danny stopped and flashed his guild card. They relaxed a fraction, but still had a trembly, wide-eyed look to them. Yeah, whatever happened, it was serious.

"What's going on, fellas?" he asked.

One of the guards shouted for the portcullis to be raised. As it began the ponderous process of clanking up out of the way, one of the others said, "Yesterday, a wizard came with six drakes. He demanded we hand over some girl. He said if we refused, he'd level the city. Six drakes and a wizard would be plenty to do the job too."

Shit! Why would the Master of Drakes go to all this effort to reclaim Liana? Surely it would be easier to just grab some other girl from the village.

Seeming completely oblivious to Danny's growing anxiety the guard continued. "Mayor Mugg handed her over and the wizard left just as peacefully as you please. We're keeping the gate shut for a bit just to be safe. Though it wouldn't do much good if the drakes did come back."

Danny wanted to rage at Mugg for giving Liana up, but in the end, no one could do anything against such a force. Anyone other than him at least. The past didn't matter in any case. He had to focus on finding a way to track her and catch up to them as quickly as possible. Hopefully he'd find what he needed at the temple.

As soon as the portcullis raised enough, Danny ducked underneath and made straight for the Goddess's temple. The walk didn't take long and about ten minutes later he pushed through the temple doors. He found the same priestess on duty and she favored him with a sad look.

"What happened?" he asked.

"She volunteered to go with the wizard in hopes of sparing the city. It was very brave. We would've protected her to the end. I hope you believe me."

Danny nodded even though he doubted their devotion to the greater good would've truly allowed them to do what the priestess claimed. As with Mugg's actions, it was irrelevant to his current problem.

"I need to find her. Did she leave anything behind? Anything I can use for a tracking spell?"

"I'll show you to her room. No one has gone in since she was taken. If there's anything you can use, take it."

Danny followed the priestess through the infirmary and down a hall. They stopped in front of an open door beyond which waited a small room, even smaller than the room Danny rented at his inn. It had a cot, a nightstand, and a trunk. He checked the trunk and found it empty. Liana hadn't exactly had time or money to accumulate possessions.

Cursing under his breath, Danny paced the room, mind racing. He stopped and snapped his fingers. Idiot! He had the answer all along. He opened his storage and pulled out the rough canvas wraps Liana had worn in place of shoes after he freed her and before he bought her real clothes.

Danny looked closely at the dirty fabric. Inch by inch he checked for what he needed. About ten yards in he found it, a spot of dried blood from a scratch he vaguely recalled healing.

Now he had to see if it was enough. Eyes closed, he called on the ether. He'd never attempted the tracking spell his host had mastered. Danny sought the resonance between Liana's blood and her body.

Seconds turned to minutes. "Come on," he muttered. "I know you're out there.

Right when he reached the verge of giving up, a faint tug pulled him toward the forest. He clenched his fist. Gotcha!

"I have to go," he told the watching priestess. "Thank you for all you've done."

She smiled, though she still looked sad. "For one touched by the Goddess, no request is too great. I wish we could've done a better job protecting Liana. Best of luck, Ronin."

He hurried out of the temple, turning right, toward the gate. He did his best not to think too hard about what she said about him being touched by the Goddess. Danny had assumed Mother Ankie recognized their connection because she was there when it happened, but maybe all of the Goddess's followers would be able to tell. If so, he'd have to take care when asking for their help since it appeared they'd be reluctant to say no.

He grimaced when he saw Mugg standing between him and the closed portcullis. A dozen guards in full armor and carrying drawn weapons flanked him.

They were no threat to Danny, but he didn't want to kill innocent men either.

"Out of the way, Guild Master."

Mugg crossed his arms. "Can't do that. If you rescue her, that lunatic sorcerer will just come back with his pet drakes to fetch her again. Maybe this time he carries out his threat to level the city."

"If you don't get out of my way, you won't have to worry about the Master of Drakes returning."

Mugg shook his head. "You know the rules. Guild members can't fight each other. If you attack me, you'll be kicked out."

Given what he'd heard about Mugg and his now-dead enforcers, Danny found his threat laughable. Besides, getting kicked out of the Adventurers' Guild would be a nuisance, but hardly one fatal to his mission.

"I'm not going to attack you," Danny said. "I'm going to walk straight ahead. If you try and stop me, you'll be the one attacking a fellow guild member."

Mugg ground his teeth and the guards tensed.

Danny took a step and they moved back to match him. "The only one who needs to worry is the Master of Drakes. When I'm finished with him, he won't be in any condition to threaten anyone ever again. Now get the hell out of my way, or you and your boys will be too dead to care what happens next."

Mugg's throat worked as he tried to swallow. He didn't back down at once, which impressed Danny. He'd imagined the man was a bigger coward.

He took another step and again the group backed up. Three more feet and their backs would hit the wall. He wouldn't actually kill them, just put them out of commission. Still, he'd prefer not to have to do that either.

After a third step Mugg said, "Stand down and open the gate."

"Mayor Mugg?" one of the guards said.

"You heard me, step aside and raise the portcullis."

Danny didn't wait for the gate to open. As soon as the guards moved out of his way, he gathered ether in his legs, ran three strides, and leapt straight over the wall. He hit the ground on the far side and took off down the road at a full sprint.

Hopefully he could catch up before the Master of Drakes did something to Liana. For everyone's sake, he needed to save her.

CHAPTER 16

For three brutal days Liana rode, bound and slung across the great one's back like a saddlebag behind the Master of Drakes. Constantly pounding against the drake's scales had left her aching to her bones. The journey had been the longest three days of her life.

But now that they'd reached their destination, a steel tower about a day north of her village, she found she wished for many more days of travel. Despite living in the forest her whole life, Liana never guessed the tower was here. Of course, anyone leaving the village seldom came back given the great ones wandering the forest. Did he plan to sacrifice her here? She'd assumed the Master of Drakes would take her to the little clearing where Ronin found her.

She should have been terrified, but instead she only felt numb. Exhaustion had smothered her fear. Which might have been a blessing in disguise.

When they came to a full stop, the Master dismounted. He pointed, and five of the great ones dispersed around the tower. She'd harbored a vague hope that Ronin might find her again, but he would have no hope against six of the great ones.

The Master looked up at her and crooked his finger. Some invisible force plucked Liana into the air and set her on her feet. Her legs trembled but she didn't collapse. She took a bit of pride in that.

"Is this where I'm to be sacrificed to the great ones?" Her voice trembled and part of her hated her weakness even as she understood it was only natural.

"No." He fixed his cold, emotionless gaze on her. "A wisp of a girl like you wouldn't even be a snack for a drake. Your life force, on the other hand, will be of considerable value to me. When I combine it with the others, I'll finally have what I need to seize control of the castle."

Liana stared at him. None of what he said made sense. At least not to her. "I don't understand."

"Nor do you need to." He gestured again and the magic pulled her along behind him as he walked toward the tower. It had no door, so she wasn't sure how they were going to go inside.

After a few silent strides he said, "I made up the story about maidens being sacrificed to please the drakes. It's the sort of thing humans find believable for some reason. As long as I got what I needed, the details were irrelevant."

"If you care so little about humans, why not just take as many as you needed in one go?" Liana couldn't believe she had the nerve to speak so boldly, but learning that everything she'd grown up taking as a fact was a lie infuriated her.

"Integrating each life force into the matrix takes time, a great deal of it. I can only add one person each year. When I brought your ancestors to the forest villages, I demanded one sacrifice every five years. That was the deal and I never break my word. The honor of an elf-blood is greater than a human could ever understand."

His explanation left Liana more confused than enlightened. They reached the blank tower wall and he touched it. A door slid up out of sight and they entered. A short walk brought them to a set of stairs leading into the earth. The dark passage sent a chill through her.

They descended, Liana's heart beating faster with each step. The air grew thick and stale. And there was something else. It reminded her of the moment before a bad thunderstorm struck.

When they reached the basement, Liana's blood turned to ice. Scores of girls around her age hung suspended from the ceiling and walls, encased in glittering, translucent crystals. Their faces were frozen in expressions of terror, eyes wide and mouths agape in silent screams. She'd never seen anything like it in her brief life, and her mind went blank.

"Heaven's mercy," she whispered. This fate was infinitely worse than being torn apart by drakes. At least that would have been quick.

The Master pointed and the magic dragged Liana to the center of the room. She wanted to run, but her limbs refused to obey. His magic held her fast, making her as helpless as a mouse in a serpent's coils.

With a lazy flick of his wrist, the same power which held her in place shredded Liana's clothes, leaving her as naked as when she was staked out for sacrifice. A glowing circle filled with complex symbols flared to life beneath her bare feet. A moment later crystal started creeping up her feet. It expanded slowly, encasing her inch by inexorable inch. Though the process didn't hurt, each second held its own special agony. Silent tears ran down her face as she gradually joined the other doomed girls.

The Master watched the process, his face an expressionless mask. When the crystals had passed her ankles, he turned, apparently satisfied, and strode out, leaving her to face her fate alone.

When she no longer heard the tread of his boots on the stairs, she allowed herself a long sob. When that did no good, she thrashed against her crystalline bonds. Her efforts yielded her nothing. The slow spread didn't change in the least, and now her hands hurt from pounding on the unbreakable crystal.

There would be no escape for her this time. No last-minute rescue by a brave warrior. This was going to be her end. Not the end she'd expected, but the end all the same.

Liana prayed to any listening archangel that Ronin would come for her after all. It was a selfish wish. He would face the jaws of the great ones and the Master's magic, but even so, she prayed.

Please, let him come and save me again.

Calum watched as the ether crystal began the slow process of assimilating Liana's body and essence. The girl was young and strong and so should provide a fine source of life force. Many so-called wizards didn't appreciate that differences in the source affected the quality and amount of life force available for extraction. Young, pure maidens provided the finest source of life force he'd ever found, which made them perfect for his purposes.

When the crystal reached her ankles, he gave a nod of

satisfaction and turned for the steps. He still remembered when he'd completed the process with the first offering. The girl's tears had troubled him, but now, having successfully repeated the process over a hundred times, he barely noticed their wailing and crying. It simply felt like part of the ritual and if it didn't happen he would've feared he'd done something wrong.

He climbed the steel staircase, his magical vision untroubled by the total darkness, and continued on until he emerged into the top chamber of the tower, a single room dominated by an intricate spell circle etched into the floor. At its center a stone pedestal grew out of the steel. It looked rather incongruous, but the stone conducted ether into his flute better than steel. Calum filed the odd fact under magic he assumed he would never understand.

And speaking of his flute, he pulled the Flute of Controlling Drakes out of its special pocket in his robes and set it on the pedestal with a magic hand. Crossing the rune physically risked damaging the magic and he'd invested far too much time to ruin it all now.

Once he had the flute in place, he offered a silent prayer to all his elven ancestors that Liana's life force would provide the power he needed to finish strengthening the flute. He raised his arms then closed his eyes before tilting his head back and fully immersing his awareness into the ether. Shimmering threads rose from the floor, wove through the spell circle, and finally coalesced at the pedestal.

All but one of them. A single thread, thin and fragile compared to the others, waved around like a headless snake. He needed to properly weave Liana's thread into the matrix before it became too dense to work with.

Calum created a set of ethereal fingers which he used to

gently, patiently, weave the new thread into the spell. It was by no means a simple or speedy process. Not only did he have to add the new thread in the right place, but he couldn't disturb any of the others in the process. But all elf-bloods had an excess of time and patience.

Beads of sweat formed on his brow as he worked, and his head began to pound before he even reached the halfway point of the first phase. Each new life added to the matrix increased the difficulty of his task, but he soldiered on, determined that nothing would stop him from achieving his final success.

Two-thirds of the way through the process, a jangling vibration ran through the wards surrounding his tower. A moment after that, the door opened. He snarled but didn't let his concentration lapse. An effort of will froze the ether, locking his progress in place.

That done, he opened his eyes and spun toward the staircase. He'd commanded the drakes to let nothing approach the tower. Six of the useless beasts surrounded the clearing and still someone had entered his home uninvited. Calum would've sworn such a thing was impossible. No one, not even the villagers, knew the location of his tower. How did some random stranger find it?

Fury twisted his normally cool features into something demonic as Calum stalked down the stairs. He'd deal with the intruder in the most painful way imaginable; a fitting punishment for anyone interfering with his masterwork.

CHAPTER 17

Danny had been exhausted plenty of times since being summoned to Valindor, but he was pretty sure he hadn't been this tired since leaving the Five Kingdoms. Thirty-six hours of nonstop running would do that to you. His whole body ached and only the many cross-country trips he took with Lyra had prepared him for such an extreme effort.

On the plus side, it seemed his effort would soon pay off. Assuming the tracking spell hadn't malfunctioned, Liana should be close. Maybe a quarter mile at most remained. Despite his eagerness, Danny forced himself to slow down. Running straight into the Master of Drakes's base without looking for traps would be beyond stupid and nudging into suicidal.

He shifted some of his magic from physical enhancement to stealth field. A couple minutes later, through a gap in the trees, a metallic glint caught his eye. Crouching for a better look, he spotted one of the elf-bloods' steel towers. This looked promising. He guessed it measured about three stories tall with no obvious door. All pretty standard for elf-bloods.

Danny crept to the very edge of the treeline and crouched. He surveyed the area, every sense enhanced to the max. Six drakes prowled the perimeter. Their forked tongues flicked out to taste the air at regular intervals. They made ugly guard dogs and he doubted Marlina's blessing would do him any good against this lot. Shifting his gaze to the tower itself, he quickly spotted the invisible rune that would let him open the door. He also spotted a simple alarm ward, but nothing dangerous.

Okay, it was a rough situation, but not impossible. With his stealth field active, Danny slipped into the clearing. He froze immediately, but the drakes gave no sign of noticing him. So far, so good.

Slow and steady, he tiptoed across the clearing, keeping well away from the drakes. His stealth field might keep him invisible and silent, but if one of the giant reptiles bumped into him, it would notice for sure.

A big, blue-scaled brute swung his way. Danny froze a moment before its tail swung through the space just ahead of him.

Sweat beaded on his brow as it lumbered clear. Once it moved out of the way, he resumed his path.

Twice more he stopped to avoid a collision, but at last he reached the tower. Sweat absolutely soaked his tunic. It stuck to his back, making it uncomfortable to move. Still, if nothing worse happened today, he'd consider himself fortunate.

When he'd caught his breath, Danny glanced over his shoulder to make sure the drakes remained a safe distance away. Satisfied, he tapped the open symbol. As soon as he did, the door slid out of the way. Danny had barely taken a step before six enraged roars split the air behind him.

He turned and slapped the inside rune to close the door. It snapped shut an instant before a dull thud sounded. A cartoonish image of one of the drakes running headfirst into it popped into his mind.

Well, he'd made it this far. Now to find Liana and deal with the Master of Drakes once and for all.

He turned away from the door to face the tower's dim interior. The only light came from the glowing door rune and it slowly faded until it grew pitch black. Danny activated a darkvision spell and the empty space resolved into shades of gray. At the back of the room, steel staircases led up and down.

From above came the clank of footsteps. Sounded like the Master of Drakes noticed his arrival. A short rest would've been nice, but he wanted to have the final battle over with so he could find Liana and move on to the ether pool.

Danny moved away from the base of the stairs to a spot off to the side where the Master of Drakes wouldn't be able to see him, opened his storage, and pulled out the ethersword.

A few steps from the bottom, a cloaked figure stopped and said, "I know you're here! Show yourself and I'll make your death a speedy one."

Danny's lips quirked up. Had anyone ever been stupid enough to give up the advantage of surprise before a firefight? He thought not and held his position. A few more steps and the target would be in range.

The Master of Drakes stepped off the bottom step and into the entry area. One more stride and he'd be able to see

Danny. Gathering himself, Danny pushed off, lit the ether-sword, and swung.

By some miracle, the target shifted aside with inches to spare.

Danny spun and slashed again, slicing the man's green robe but missing the flesh beneath.

The Master sprang back, putting a few feet between them. Danny's exhaustion from his long run kept him from using anything close to his maximum body strengthening. Not wanting to run headlong into a trap, he eased closer, alert for any sign of a spell forming.

Instead of attacking, the Master said, "You must be Ronin. You've caused me a great deal of trouble."

Danny nodded, his gaze never wavering. "It was my pleasure."

"So what's your price?"

Danny cocked his head. "Price?"

"To go away and forget you ever met Liana. I know your kind. Humans care only about acquiring wealth. I have some gems and other trinkets. I'll let you kill a couple of my drakes and take their bodies. That would be enough to make you rich, would it not?"

"I'm already rich. Here's my counteroffer. Release Liana and give me the Flute of Controlling Drakes. Do that and I'll let you walk away."

"It seems we're at an impasse," the Master said.

Danny shrugged. "I never thought we were going to be able to come to an understanding."

He charged the mithril hilt with ether and punched forward, sending a fist of power rushing at the Master.

The Master's defense crumpled and he flew back to slam into the tower wall.

Danny advanced as the Master slowly climbed to his feet. That spell had taken a fair bit of Danny's remaining strength. If this dragged on too much longer, he was going to be in trouble.

Well, worse trouble.

Two yards out Danny sprang and swung a diagonal slash.

The Master dodged back, but too slowly. His right hand fell to the floor with a spurt of blood. A pained shout preceded a blinding flash of light.

Danny looked away and conjured the strongest barrier his weakened state would allow. When the light faded, he watched the Master flee through the tower's open door. It slid shut before Danny had a chance to cast another spell. He didn't think about trying to follow. Even at full strength he wouldn't have wanted to fight six drakes. Right now, staying on his feet took all his willpower; any pursuit would have to wait.

Swallowing his frustration, Danny deactivated the ether-sword and put it back in storage. He'd call this round a draw. Now, if he was an insane elf-blood wizard, where would he keep his prisoners?

A humorless smile twisted his lips. Likely the same place every evil asshole Danny had met kept them: the basement.

With weary steps, Danny descended into the tower's lower level. At least his darkvision spell didn't take much effort to maintain. Nothing troubled him as he walked and soon he reached the bottom.

What he found stole his breath. Scores, maybe hundreds, of young women hung from the ceiling or grew out of the walls, their bodies entombed in crystals and their faces frozen in eternal anguish. In the center of the floor, Liana stood in the middle of a spell circle, crystal having grown over everything below her armpits.

He stayed silent, studying the magic as he sought a way to free her. After a couple minutes he gave up trying to make sense of the complex spells. A thin thread rose from the top of Liana's head and vanished up through the ceiling. If this tower followed the same layout as the other elf-blood towers he'd visited, he'd find another spell circle on the top floor connected to this one.

Danny finally conjured a light. While Liana squinted at him, he moved closer. "Hey. How come every time I rescue you, someone has taken your clothes off?"

She started crying. "Ronin. I prayed you'd come for me. The Master..."

"Run off, unfortunately. I wasn't strong enough to beat him, but I did get a hand off of him. Looks like the crystal's stopped growing. On the downside, I have no idea how to reverse the process." Maybe he shouldn't have admitted that, but Danny wouldn't lie to her. Liana deserved better.

"What are you going to do?" Liana asked in a trembling, terrified voice.

"Not abandon you, if that's what you're worried about. I am going to go upstairs and see if I can figure out how this spell works from the other end. Though given its complexity, I'm not optimistic. Assuming I can't sort it out myself, once I recover my strength, I'll see if Marlina can help."

"Who?" Liana asked.

"Marlina, the Queen of the Forest. She's a greater drake and older than the elf-bloods who made this place. Hopefully she'll know something useful."

"Why would she help us?" Liana asked.

"She owes me a favor," Danny said. "And even if she didn't, I suspect she'd help simply because she's a good person. Anyway, first things first. I'm going upstairs. Can I do anything for you before I go?"

"I can't feel my body anymore." She sniffed. "Only my face works for the moment. I'll be fine. Go, do what you can. And thank you for coming for me."

"Don't thank me until I finish the job." Danny headed for the steps. Every stride took his full focus. He dearly wanted to rest, but with no way to seal the tower, he refused to risk the Master of Drakes sneaking back in and attacking while he was unconscious.

Climbing to the third floor took far more physical and mental effort than it should've, but somehow he made it to the top without falling on his face. What he found didn't encourage him in the least. The spell circle covering the floor looked every bit as complex as the one downstairs. The Master had woven all the threads from the girls below into the circle. He assumed they represented the girls' life forces. If Danny had been inclined to optimism, he might've thought it meant they still lived, but he refused to get his hopes up.

A stone pedestal rose out of the center of the circle and on it rested a flute formed of silver metal. Ether ran through the flute, starting at the mouthpiece and emerging from the front. Looked like less of a flute and more like a typical elf-blood magical item. As far as he could tell, it worked the same way as his ethersword.

Danny held out a hand and a tentacle of ether pulled the flute to him. He tried using it to enhance the strength of his magic and failed, thus confirming it was made of actual silver and not mithril. He created a plug of dense ether and used it to cover the opening of the flute. Over about ten seconds the flow of ether from the other end ceased. That should've freed the drakes outside.

Only one way to find out for sure and right now he was too tired to test his theory. Eager as Danny was to free Liana, he needed to get some sleep before he tried anything else. He'd make easy prey for any beast in the forest given his current condition. The situation appeared stable for the moment. A long nap should be safe. And even if it wasn't, at this point he needed to sleep before he passed out. The second floor looked like living quarters. Getting some shuteye in the Master of Drakes's own bed held a certain ironic appeal.

He took a moment to set a basic but lethal ward on the tower door. That done, it didn't take long to find the bedroom and he soon settled into a wonderfully soft feather bed and zonked out in seconds.

Calum fled from his tower, cradling the bleeding stump of his severed wrist against his chest as he went. A tourniquet conjured from pure ether reduced the flow of blood to almost nothing. Pain and shock drove him through his exhaustion. His only thought was to put as much distance between himself and the man who did this to him as possible. Calum's mind reeled when he thought about what just happened.

How had a mere human defeated him in combat? Him, an elf-blood wizard with centuries of experience? The wretch couldn't have been more than eighteen. It was unthinkable.

And yet the searing pain shooting up his arm served as undeniable proof. Calum hated humans in general, but he was developing an especially intense hatred of this one. His life wouldn't be complete until he made Ronin pay for the many insults the human had forced him to endure.

And even worse than losing to a human, he'd been forced to abandon the Flute of Controlling Drakes. Without it, he was vulnerable. The drakes guarding his tower had let him pass unharmed thanks to its lingering power, but out here in the wild reaches of the forest, should he have the misfortune to run into any of the wild drakes who called the forest home, he was fair game.

How pathetic for a wizard of his lineage to be brought to such a miserable state. His ancestors would be disgusted if they saw him now, fleeing like a frightened rabbit.

But he had no other choice.

He needed time to recover his strength and plan his revenge. And for that, he needed somewhere safe to hole up and heal. Luckily for him, he'd planned for this unlikely turn of events long ago.

The first human village he'd established had an emergency workshop. The humans all knew better than to enter the building. He'd fed one overly curious fellow to the drakes and the rest learned quickly, like properly trained animals.

Hours blurred by as he stumbled through the shadowed woods, senses straining for any hint of an approaching drake. He'd been reasonably confident that he'd taken the beast which claimed this part of the forest as one of the guardians of his tower, but exhaustion left his mind so blurry he didn't fully trust his memory.

Weariness dragged at him. The aftereffects of the grueling

magical ritual combined with blood loss and the constant pain from his maimed arm left him in a daze, stumbling along, only vaguely aware of his location and destination.

At last, as darkness settled over the forest, the trees thinned and he caught a glimpse of thatch roofs. The village. Finally.

Jaw clenched, he reached deep for the focus necessary to weave an invisibility spell. The last thing he wanted was for any of the villagers to see him arrive in this pitiful state. The wretched humans might get ideas. And right now he lacked the strength to defend himself from one human with a shovel, much less a village full of them.

Once the magic settled into place, Calum lurched onward. Fortunately he'd built the simple house that served as his backup workshop on the very edge of the village, which made it easier to avoid curious eyes.

His skin tingled when he passed through the outer ward and reached for the front door. The magic was keyed to allow him entry without requiring anything else. And thank goodness for that.

Inside, the main room swam before his eyes. He focused on the chest in the corner of the nearly empty room that held his cache of supplies. He dropped to his knees and threw the lid open. All manner of healing equipment filled the space. He grabbed a poultice pretreated with healing herbs and wrapped it around the oozing stump of his right wrist. It was an awkward job with his off hand. The shaking of his fingers didn't help either.

When the medicine finally kicked in, blessed numbness spread through his arm, reducing the pain to a bearable throb. The room started spinning and he staggered like a drunk toward the back room where his bed waited. He barely made it before his legs gave out.

As he collapsed onto the thin, musty-smelling mattress, a final thought flickered through his weary mind. No matter what it took, he would reclaim his tower and make Ronin pay.

CHAPTER 18

Danny woke up in a haze. Where was he and why was he sleeping on the softest, most comfortable mattress he'd found since leaving the Five Kingdoms? As he sat up and looked around at the unfamiliar bedroom, everything came rushing back. Right, this was the Master of Drakes's tower. He fought the prick but he got away. Hopefully that all happened yesterday and he hadn't slept through a full day. His muscles protested when he rolled out of bed, but at least everything still worked properly.

His stomach snarled that it was time for breakfast. Though he generally preferred not to cook using magic, he had no interest in finding and figuring out how the kitchen here worked. So, after a few minutes of prep, he had bacon sizzling in his pan over a conjured flame. The indescribably glorious smell filled the air and when it finished crisping up, he warmed some biscuits in the hot grease. Once they got nice and toasty, he made a couple sandwiches and devoured them.

Meal complete, he made his way down to the basement. Liana remained exactly as he left her, encased in crystal up to her armpits. He let out a breath of relief when he found the crystal hadn't moved any further. Danny feared that he hadn't succeeded in stopping the ritual. Now he needed to figure out how to reverse the process.

"Morning. At least I think it's morning," Danny said. "How are you feeling?"

"The same, numb where the crystal is touching. Nothing seems to be working down there. I'm not hungry or thirsty." Her cheeks flushed. "I don't have to go to the outhouse."

"That's a good thing, given your situation. I'm going to Marlina's castle. Hopefully she'll know how to free you. It's about a day's run from here, so I shouldn't be gone for too long."

Her eyes widened. "What if he comes back while you're gone?"

Liana didn't have to specify who she meant. "Don't worry about him. I'm going to ward the door with the strongest magic I've got. I'll be back way before he can break through it. Okay?"

She managed a weak nod. "Go on. I'm basically dead anyway."

"Don't talk like that. As long as you're breathing, there's hope. Believe it." He moved closer and brushed her tears away. "Look at me."

She lifted her head.

"We'll figure something out. Have a little faith, in heaven if not in me."

Her lips quirked up in a sad smile. "I have far more faith in you than heaven. Good luck."

"I'll take all I can get." After a final reassuring touch of her cheek, he turned and jogged back up the stairs.

In the entry chamber, he paused to grab the Master's hand then he walked over to the door and pressed the rune. The door slid out of sight. In the clearing, a lone drake sprawled on the grass, blue scales glinting in the morning light. Danny took the ethersword out of storage and slipped outside. The drake shot him a look of bored disinterest before resuming its basking.

No aggression, no attack.

Looked like Marlina's blessing still protected him. Even better, shutting off the flow of ether to the flute had freed the drake from the Master's control. At least something had gone right.

Danny exhaled and turned his back to the drake to focus on the door. When it slid shut, he wove the strongest lethal ward he knew around it and gave the spell plenty of power. Anyone wanting to enter the tower would have to earn it.

With the tower as secure as he could make it, he returned the ethersword to storage. He had to check one more thing before he began the long run to Marlina's castle. Danny used the same tracking spell that led him to Liana to search for the Master of Drakes. The spell activated, but something blocked the magic. Well, he hadn't been all that optimistic. A wizard as powerful as the Master no doubt knew many ways to conceal his presence.

Danny shrugged and tossed the hand away. Time to get this show on the road. Now that the drakes were free from the Master's control, nothing would slow him down on his run to the castle.

Near dawn the next day Danny reached the clearing surrounding the castle. He'd taken a four-hour nap a little after midnight which did wonders to restore his strength.

A quick glance around confirmed nothing had changed during his absence. When he looked at the dark stone structure, it gave the impression of something forever unchanging. He shook off the foolish thought. When he finally destroyed the ether pool, the energy released would blow the castle to smithereens along with everything else in the area. Since confirming it had been used as a prison to trap his friend's mother, he didn't feel too bad about leveling the place.

Danny paused and took a few deep breaths. Despite the extended journey, he still felt pretty good. Maybe his time in this world was making him stronger, honing his endurance. The desperate need driving him forward probably helped too.

As he approached, the castle's massive doors swung open and Marlina emerged. She wore the same beautiful black dress as the last time he saw her. Danny was pretty sure it was part of her magical transformation rather than an actual garment. She walked to the very edge of her binding and stopped, also the same as last time.

Danny pulled the flute out of storage. "I deactivated it. Was that enough to free you?"

Marlina shook her head, her expression unreadable. "No. Until it's destroyed, I'm still bound to protect the castle. Were you planning to use it to make me do something?"

Danny stared, unable to speak for a moment. "What? No, of course not."

He grabbed the ethersword, lit it, tossed the flute in the

air, and sliced it cleanly in two. "I was just curious if deactivating it would be enough."

A stunning smile broke across Marlina's face, transforming her cold beauty into something warm and approachable. "With your power, you could've used that flute to seize control of every drake in the forest. You could've commanded an army capable of conquering half the continent."

Danny snorted and shook his head. "During my time in the military, I was in charge of six other guys. Keeping them all focused and moving in the right direction nearly drove me nuts. Ruling half a continent sounds like a nightmare, not a dream."

Marlina's laugh reminded him of silvery bells. "You are an odd human, Daniel."

"You're not the first to say so. Did it work?"

She took another step and spun in a circle, her dress swirling around her. "Yes, I'm free after all these years. I can't begin to know how to thank you."

"I'm glad to help, but if you wanted to do something to pay me back, I've got a hundred-odd girls imprisoned in crystal and no idea how to free them without killing them. The Master of Drakes trapped them under his tower. Would you mind taking a look?"

"Absolutely. I have some skill with magic and my time in the castle gave me plenty of time to study elf-blood spells. Let's go and see what can be done."

Danny blew out a breath he hadn't realized he was holding. "Awesome. It took me most of a day to run here. After I rest a bit, I'll show you to the tower."

"Getting back will be considerably faster." Marlina's form shimmered and, in a heartbeat, a massive drake stood before him, her scales gleaming flame red in the morning light. Merrok had been huge and she was half again as big as him.

Climb on. Marlina's telepathic voice startled him. *I'll fly us there.*

Danny gathered ether in his legs and sprang up on her back, settling himself between her wings. A band of ether secured him in place and a moment later Marlina launched herself skyward. Huge wings beat hard, sending gusts of wind every which way.

The flight back to the tower went far faster than his run, and a couple hours after leaving the castle, they arrived. The lone drake hadn't moved, so Danny assumed this was its territory. It lowered its head in the drake equivalent of a bow as Marlina landed.

Danny slid off her back. His boots had barely hit the ground before she was standing beside him in human form again. It seemed like magic that powerful should take longer, but then again he'd never seen shapeshifting magic like this before, so what did he know?

A few strides from the door Danny waved his hand, dispelling the ward he'd set. No one had messed with it during his absence. Good, hopefully the Master of Drakes hadn't recovered from his wound yet.

"I didn't know this tower was here," Marlina said. "The elf-bloods must've built it after they bound me to the castle."

"They were industrious people, no doubt about that. I keep running into these steel buildings everywhere I go. Most of them had power-hungry assholes living in them."

"Every wizard is on the lookout for some lost secret which might increase their power even a fraction. So it has always been and likely it will always be."

Danny found the thought depressing. He opened the door and conjured a light. "The spell circle is on the third floor."

She nodded and followed him up the stairs in silence.

When they reached the third floor, Marlina immediately went to the spell circle. Danny kept his distance and his peace. He'd learned during his brief time on this world that rushing magical analysis never turned out well.

At last she said, "I can reverse the weaving, but I'll need your help."

Danny wasn't great at delicate magic, but he nodded. "Just tell me what to do."

"Look closely. Do you see that one thread sort of flailing around? I need you to hold it steady while I pick it out of the matrix. If it hits something it shouldn't, it'll cause a chain reaction which might kill all the captured humans."

That sounded simple enough that even Danny could manage it. He conjured a hand of ether and grasped the thread, holding it still.

"Good, just like that." Marlina got to work, picking and prodding, until finally the thread came free. "You can let it go."

He did and the thread sank back out of sight.

"I have to check on Liana."

"Good idea," Marlina said. "If she came through it unscathed, there's a good chance the rest of them will as well."

Danny hurried downstairs, eager to see if their efforts had paid off. A few steps from the bottom he paused and took a breath. There was no guarantee this worked. He needed a moment to mentally prepare himself for the worst possibility.

When he'd readied himself, he took the final three steps

and conjured a light. Liana stood there, on her own, brushing shards of crystal from her bare skin. It worked, thank goodness.

Liana turned to face him, squinting against the glare. Tears leaked down her cheeks and she sniffed.

Danny hurried over and she hugged him. "It's okay. You're safe now."

When she stopped crying he gently disentangled himself and reached into his storage for the same spare tunic she'd worn before. "Here."

Liana pulled it on and smiled. "Thanks, for everything. I was sure I was going to die down here..."

She trailed off and stiffened.

Danny turned to find Marlina standing beside the door, her gaze sweeping over the other crystal-encased girls. "This is awful. I never imagined he'd go so far to gain access to the castle."

"Ronin, who's she?" Liana asked.

"Right, sorry. Liana, this is Marlina, she's a greater fire drake and the Queen of the Forest. She was kind enough to help unravel the Master of Drakes's magic. I'm not sure what I would've done if she hadn't agreed to lend a hand."

"A queen?" Liana said. "I didn't know the forest had a queen. Um, thank you, Your Majesty."

"Marlina, please. I'm queen of the drakes, not of the humans." She turned to Danny, her expression grave. "Freeing the others will be more difficult. When the crystals shatter, they'll fall. They could easily break their necks."

"Can you manage to free them without me?" Danny asked. "I can stay down here and catch them."

Marlina nodded. "That should work. Since the others are fully integrated into the matrix, their threads won't react as freely as Liana's life force would've. Freeing them all will not be a speedy process."

"The ether pool has been there for fifteen hundred years. It'll keep for a few more days."

"An odd human indeed." He barely made out Marlina's murmured words before she went back up the stairs.

"What are we going to do?" Liana asked.

"What do you mean?"

"I mean I don't think the temple can find places for all of us. Assuming they survive, the first sacrifices will be over a hundred years old. Everyone they knew is long dead. I'm not sure the villages will welcome us back. Our survival, from their point of view, violates the villages' founding deals."

"I don't know what to tell you," Danny said. "When we finish here, we'll worry about what comes next. All I can promise is to do my best for all of you."

A crack sounded from above, ending the discussion. Danny swallowed a sigh. Helping all these women may well end up being harder than dealing with the plague.

Either way, he'd do his best and hope it sufficed.

CHAPTER 19

Calum winced as he applied a pungent salve to the raw stump of his right wrist. He gritted his teeth against the pain and focused on his work. He'd slept for a full day and now his magic had recovered. Pity he could do nothing about the lost hand, but at least the healing salve would prevent infection from setting in by quickly growing a fresh layer of skin over the wound. If he had access to his tower, he'd have more options, but even he lacked the power to grow a new hand.

His hand slipped and some of the amber goop splattered on the floor. He swallowed a curse. Learning to use his left hand for everything wasn't going to be easy either. Damn Ronin! One way or another he swore he'd make the human pay for this insult.

Calum carefully wrapped a clean bandage around the stump. In a few hours the salve would do its work, but until then he needed to keep the wound clean. Once he had the bandage in place, he conjured a second ethereal hand and tied it off. With that taken care of, he considered his next problem. In addition to his hand, Ronin had taken the Flute of Controlling Drakes. Without it, Calum had no way to command the forest drakes. Which meant he had no hope of raising a force to help him retake his tower.

For a moment he considered conscripting the villagers, but any number of humans armed with farm implements would be of no use. A single spell would wipe them out in an instant. And the idea of them fighting a drake was even more ludicrous. They wouldn't be able to scratch it, much less do any serious damage.

Shouts of alarm outside interrupted his plotting. What in the world could've happened to stir the vermin up? Nothing interesting ever happened in these villages. He'd set them up to be safe and boring for the humans. Not because he cared about their wellbeing, but rather to avoid having to find replacements. Plus, he'd promised them a safe place to live as part of the deal that assured him a steady supply of sacrifices and Calum always honored his word, even when he gave it to lesser beings.

Equal parts intrigued and annoyed, Calum stepped outside, careful to keep his maimed hand hidden within the folds of his robe. A cluster of terrified villagers stood in the middle of the village's lone street as they gesticulated wildly at the sky. When they finally noticed his presence they prostrated themselves.

He pointed at one of them. "What is the meaning of this ruckus?"

"Master, a massive red drake just flew by the village." The human pointed toward the castle. "It came from that way."

Calum's heart raced. The drake bound to the castle matched that description. Assuming he was right, someone—Ronin's hated face popped into his mind only to be quickly banished—must've broken the binding. That meant he should have a clear path to seize the castle for himself.

Heaven hadn't abandoned Calum after all. His hard work and suffering weren't for nothing. He would claim the castle's secrets and use them to grind Ronin under his boot.

Without another word, Calum marched out of the village.

"Master! What about the drake? What should we do?"

He ignored the human and picked up his pace. Calum had to reach the castle before the drake returned from her errand. Assuming she ever did. Now that someone had broken the binding, who knew what she might do.

No, best to assume the worst and reach the castle as quickly as possible. Which, he hated to admit, was a good deal slower than he would've managed at his best.

Days of constant running left Calum exhausted, but when he finally strode into the clearing surrounding the castle everything still appeared abandoned. Looked like he'd made it here first. The pain in his severed wrist throbbed in time with his heartbeat. The injury didn't appreciate the rough treatment and it informed him of its displeasure in no uncertain terms.

He ignored the pain and approached the castle. At any moment he expected the door to open and the beautiful guardian to appear. But she didn't and at last he stood before the closed doors. He sensed no wards. Odd, but then again, considering the power of the guardian they left behind, his ancestors probably figured they'd be pointless.

The wood felt cold and rough under his palm. He'd been waiting so long to make the castle his own. Despite his urgent need to hurry, he closed his eyes and savored the moment. This was his reward for centuries of effort. No matter what, he refused to rush.

When the moment passed, he pulled the doors open and stepped inside. His footsteps echoed in the cavernous foyer. The interior looked like a near mirror image of his own tower, steel walls devoid of decorations, bare floors, and nothing resembling a personality to be seen. He expected to find something warmer. Instead he found a typical elf-blood fortress that his ancestors gave a castle's exterior on a whim. He couldn't begin to imagine why they'd go through the effort. In the end, elf-bloods were as diverse in their thinking and tastes as humans.

Calum began searching on the first floor. He checked each room but found little of interest. Dust cloths draped over the occasional piece of furniture. A couple of rooms had fireplaces but no wood. The whole thing brought to mind someone who didn't know what a castle should look like, but had tried to make one. On the second floor he finally found something interesting, the library.

Hundreds of books filled dozens of shelves. He'd been dreaming of this moment since he learned the fortress existed. He strolled around, checking each row, glancing at spines to try and get an idea of the library's contents. The titles didn't provide great clues since they tended to emphasize the author's name rather than the subject. No doubt someone familiar with the many different authors would be better served by the naming system than Calum, who hadn't heard of any of them.

As he walked up the rightmost aisle, he spotted a stone statue tucked into an out-of-the-way corner. Judging by the severe, angular features and pointed ears, it was an elf-blood.

Calum had never seen one of his ancestors depicted in a full statue before. Elf-bloods, in his experience, had little use for art.

He moved closer to examine the inscription on the base. A foot from the statue a voice asked, "You are of our blood?"

"Yes." He answered without hesitation.

A faint click provided the only warning before the floor dropped beneath his feet. He plunged down a hidden chute through the darkness, sliding along a smooth steel tube until it leveled out and he began to slow. A bright square appeared ahead of him, growing gradually larger.

A few seconds later the chute ended with Calum coming to a gentle rest on the edge of the exit opening. He stood and winced. The unexpected impacts hadn't done his wrist any good.

Satisfied that the damage had been minimal, Calum took a long look around the room he found himself in. The laboratory held all manner of magical and alchemical devices, all of them perfectly clean and ready for use. Five vats lined the back wall. A number of workbenches, some covered with alchemy equipment and others carved with complex spell circles, were positioned around the room at regular intervals. The space made Calum's own workshop seem like a child's playroom in comparison.

He pushed away from the wall and moved further into the room, eager to explore the many wonders on display. Barely three steps later a spectral figure materialized in front of him. The ghost was a perfect twin of the statue above. He sensed no corruption from the spirit, which meant it wasn't undead. Assuming he was correct, Calum had no idea what he'd run into.

"Who are you?" the spirit asked.

"Calum Thorne. Who are you?"

"I was Tharion Dusk. Though if you're speaking to me here, it means I died at some point. No doubt during the council's stupid invasion mission. I argued against it but they ignored my advice."

Calum stared, dumbfounded. The Dusk clan was well known among elf-bloods as one of the leading families during the height of the empire. Tharion had served as the clan's head and a member of the council. This castle had to be one of his private research facilities. In his most optimistic dreams Calum never imagined this would be such an important location.

"Did you free my guardian? I felt her binding shatter not long ago."

"No, Lord Dusk. I planned to seize control of her, but a human adventurer interrupted my plans. He seized the flute and, I'm forced to assume, found some way to use it to free the drake."

"How... disappointing. This human must've destroyed my flute. Nothing else would've broken the binding."

Calum stared, struck dumb once more. Ronin destroyed such a powerful magical relic? Why would the fool do such a thing? The flute made its wielder tremendously powerful. To destroy something so valuable beggared imagination. Even worse, it meant Calum wouldn't be able to reclaim the artifact for himself.

"But," Lord Dusk's spirit said. "I see that you are wounded. Here we are chatting as if all is well while you suffer. Allow me to repair your arm. You'll need to be at your best if you're to defeat this human when he arrives."

A little frown twisted Calum's lips. He knew of no magic capable of regenerating a hand. Then he remembered to whom he spoke. What Calum knew about magic no doubt amounted to the faintest shadow of Lord Dusk's vast wisdom. And he was right. The only reason for Ronin to free the drake was so he could enter the castle.

"What do I have to do?"

One of the cylinders along the wall slid open in the center with the top rising into the ceiling and the bottom dropping into the floor. "Get in. I'll handle the rest."

Calum approached the indicated cylinder, but hesitated. "Are there risks?"

The spirit laughed. "How long have you been a wizard? Have you found any sort of magic without risks? If you wish a new hand, this is the only way. Choose."

He was right of course. Magic and risk went hand in hand if you wished to accomplish anything and Calum very much wanted to restore what he'd lost. A wizard with one hand faced a severe handicap.

"So be it." He stepped into the cylinder and it clunked shut.

As soon as the two halves were linked, crimson fluid began to rise out of the floor. It rapidly reached his knees, then his waist. When it reached his neck, Calum started to panic.

"Wait! I'll drown!"

"Calm yourself." Lord Dusk's voice held a hint of contempt. "You will not suffocate. Once the solution enters your lungs, you can breathe it as easily as air."

Calum fought down his panic. Lord Dusk had no reason to want him dead. They shared the same blood, though Calum came from a different line. Steeling himself as the liquid covered his mouth, he took a deep breath.

He'd seldom experienced a stranger feeling than the

liquid filling his lungs, but once he got used to it, he found that it worked very much like breathing air. He cursed himself for his weakness and lack of faith. Soon he would be restored and nothing else mattered.

A faint tingling ran through the stump of his right hand and a moment later a tiny, inhuman finger ending in a sharp claw poked out through the bandage. He had just long enough to be confused when a wave of agony unlike anything he'd ever experienced washed over him.

CHAPTER 20

The crackle of shattering crystal filled the chamber beneath the Master of Drakes's tower. When the girl trapped inside finally came free, Danny caught her on a cushion of ether before lowering her gently to the floor. Marlina had already freed the ones attached to the ceiling and they were now working their way around the walls. She'd freed over a hundred girls during the past five days and the tower was getting crowded. Liana handled explaining the situation to the freed girls which suited Danny fine. He figured it would be better for them to hear from their fellow villager rather than a stranger.

Another problem had been clothes, specifically that none of the girls had any. He'd ended up raiding the closet in the living area on the second floor. He cut up every scrap of cloth in the tower into tube tops and skirts just long enough to preserve their modesty. Not exactly a great solution, but it beat having a hundred naked girls running around the tower. There should be just enough cloth left for the remaining few girls.

The most recently rescued girl sat up and groaned. She looked around as if uncertain where she found herself or what happened to her. Since she'd likely been trapped in that crystal for over a century, the lack of any worse problems than a screwed-up memory had to be some kind of miracle. And as far as he could tell, she was a perfectly healthy teenager. None of the girls had any issues with their general health. It looked like when the crystal closed over them, time stopped.

Liana hurried over with an outfit for the new girl. The white cloth came from a cut-up bedsheet. As soon as he finished confirming the girl's health, he looked away to give her some privacy.

"Excuse me," a hesitant voice said.

He turned a fraction to find one of the girls from, he was pretty sure, yesterday a few steps away. "What's on your mind?"

"Food. Everyone's getting hungry."

"Right, no problem. As soon as Marlina's ready to take a break, I'll fix something. It won't be fancy. I don't have the supplies for that."

She hastened to wave her hands. "Anything is fine, thank you. Since I came out of the crystal, all I want to do is eat and sleep. That's strange, isn't it? After being asleep for so long, you'd think I'd be full of energy."

Danny didn't think explaining she'd basically had the life sucked out of her for the past few decades and that was bound to leave you worn out would do anything to make her feel better. Instead he said, "Your body knows what it needs. Take it slow and don't try to push yourself. You've got plenty of time."

She smiled, revealing teeth far too perfect for a world

without orthodontics and reminding him once again that on Earth, all of these girls would've been able to find work as models. Such a concentration of hot girls shouldn't be possible, but his eyes assured him that it was, in fact, very much possible.

Another crack sounded and he hurried to move into position. Five minutes later the latest girl stood safely on the ground. Once again Danny confirmed that she, like the rest, had no lingering health issues, and he waved Liana over. She collected a top and skirt and hurried to join him. "We're almost done. I can't believe it, but it looks like everyone's going to be okay. That has to be a miracle."

Danny couldn't argue with that. "Did you have a chance to speak with the girls from your village?"

"A little. Some of them are angry, but most are scared of what their families will say when they come home."

"I'm not surprised. Which camp do you fall into?"

"Both, I guess. Whenever I think about how they handed me over without a second thought I get angry, then I remember what would've happened to the village if they refused the Master of Drakes's orders and it's hard to stay mad. I just want to get back to something like a normal life. Do you think that's possible?"

"I think anything's possible, but it won't be easy. I'll do what I can, but ultimately it's up to you and the others to figure out what you want to do with your lives."

Daniel, I'm taking a break.

"Marlina's done for the moment," Danny said. "I'm going upstairs to see about a meal."

"Once I get the new girl sorted out, I'll come up and give you a hand."

"No need. You've been working like crazy. A break would do you good. I'll Shanghai a couple of the others to help with slicing and chopping. I'm making bean soup again, so it won't take much other than patience."

She looked disappointed, but didn't say anything as she turned her attention to the gradually recovering girl on the floor. Danny recognized her growing attachment to him and he was trying his best to dissuade her without being unkind. Once he concluded his business in the Forest of Drakes, he planned to move on and he couldn't take Liana with him. She wouldn't last a day on the road at his best normal pace, much less his magically enhanced sprint. The sooner she got used to the idea that they'd be parting company in the near future, the better.

Danny left the basement and hurried up to the second floor. On the landing he found Marlina waiting. She looked every bit as beautiful as when he saw her that first day at the castle. If all the casting she'd done had taken any toll on her, it didn't show.

"Hey, how are you holding up?" he asked.

"Well, thank you. Pacing myself makes a huge difference. When we resume, I believe I'll be able to free the remaining victims. Everyone I remove from the matrix makes the process that much easier. Have there been issues with this batch?"

"Though I have a hard time believing it, everyone's perfectly healthy. Their mental state is a bit fragile, but whose wouldn't be under these circumstances? I'm getting dinner started." Danny frowned. "You know, I don't think I've seen you eat anything since we arrived."

"Drakes survive mainly on ethereal energy. Lesser drakes

need more meat than greater drakes, but they can go months between meals. It's one of the reasons so many of us can live in the forest without depleting the ecosystem."

He hadn't thought about that specifically, but when she pointed it out, it made perfect sense. "Speaking of the ecosystem, how will my destroying the ether pool affect it?"

"The ethereal concentration will lessen and many of the drakes will drift off to other territories. Overall it won't have a negative impact." She smiled an enigmatic smile. "What would you do if I said destroying it would have a horrible effect on us?"

Danny respected Marlina enough not to lie. "I don't know. Technically I only have to destroy eleven of the ether pools to render the summoning spell unusable, so I could leave this one alone if I absolutely had to. That said, I'm glad it won't be an issue."

She laughed. "You're too kindhearted for your own good. Eventually you're going to find yourself in a situation where you have to choose between two opposing, but equally honorable options. You need to decide how important your goal is to you before reaching that point."

Marlina wasn't wrong, but Danny couldn't make such a decision preemptively.

"Then again," she said. "Your basic decency is charming. In fact, I think it's what I like best about you."

So saying she brushed past him and kissed his cheek before continuing down to the first floor. He touched the spot she kissed. Her lips were warmer than a human woman's, but by no means unpleasant. He didn't appreciate the irony that he'd found a woman he could be with—drakes and humans weren't genetically compatible, according to the

Wizards' Guild's book—but she was his friend's mother. On any world, them hooking up would not be cool.

He shook his head and shoved the thought down deep. He needed to start dinner. The rest of his problems would keep until later.

CHAPTER 21

Danny and Marlina led the line of girls through the forest to the nearest human village. It felt so strange, walking at the speed of a normal person. He'd gotten so used to running everywhere it seemed like they were making no progress. They freed the last girl yesterday afternoon and, while Danny would've very much preferred to give them more time to recover, he barely had enough food for one more meal. He'd cleaned out the tower's larder and cooked all but half a pound of bacon, seven strips of jerky and two biscuits out of his own supplies. Getting everyone to some sort of civilization before they starved took priority.

Behind them, soft voices murmured as they discussed, he assumed, their future. Danny had an idea he thought might work if everyone agreed. Marlina glided along beside him, all grace and beauty. She showed no ill effects from all the magic she'd used over the last week. Given what he'd seen, he suspected her skill at magic far outstripped his. He also thought she was one of those individuals the Reaper mentioned who was stronger than him.

All things considered, he was very glad they ended up as friends.

"You keep sneaking looks at me," Marlina said. "If something's on your mind, please share."

"And here I thought I was being subtle. I've been trying to think of a way to ask you for another favor after all you've already done without seeming greedy."

"Ask," she said. "Worst-case scenario, I say no and you're right back where you started. Then again, I might say yes."

When she put it that way, what the hell. "Can you tell the drakes not to attack humans? Without the Master's magic to protect them, the villages might be in danger. Also, I was thinking of introducing the Wizards' Guild to them and seeing if they could cultivate the herbs that the wizards value. Assuming it was safe for them to travel between Scale City and the villages, it would be a good source of income and a way to start integrating the isolated people into broader society."

"You've given this a lot of thought," Marlina said.

"I've had a lot of time to think. I basically showed up and turned these people's world upside down. I have some responsibility for helping them get things stabilized. At least I feel like I do. It might all fall apart, but if I can offer them your protection and the potential for trade, maybe that works out for everyone. It's a starting point anyway."

"I can tell the drakes not to attack, but if the humans do anything aggressive, they will defend themselves."

Danny grinned. "Any human stupid enough to attack a drake deserves to get eaten. How smart are the lesser drakes anyway? I tried to talk my way out of a fight with a lesser earth drake, but it wouldn't listen to me and I ended up having to kill it. I assume that was because it was under the flute's control."

"They're very smart," Marlina said. "Their inability to communicate with humans verbally or telepathically makes them seem less intelligent. But they can understand human speech and are generally uninterested in fighting as long as they or their eggs aren't threatened."

"Good to know. I feared they might be more aggressive. If they're not, it makes me more confident that my plan will work, assuming the villagers are interested. In my experience, if someone is going to cause problems, it'll be the human side. And I include elf-bloods in that since they're at least half human and it shows."

"That's a rather negative view of your species," Marlina said.

"How many humans have you met?" Danny asked. "I've met plenty, some good and many more not good. I take some solace in knowing that there aren't too many really evil people, but greedy, stupid, and arrogant? We've got those to spare."

She touched his shoulder and Danny sighed. He really needed to stop saying things like that, even if it was the truth. Most people disliked hearing it.

They continued on mostly in silence for the rest of the day, taking an occasional break, but generally keeping up a steady pace until they emerged from the forest in view of a little village filled with thatched huts and surrounded by fields. Not exactly what you expected to see hundreds of miles deep in a forest. People were trudging in from the fields when one of them noticed Danny and his companions. They pointed then shouted and soon a group armed with hoes and pitchforks had formed up in the middle of the village's lone road.

They looked ready to charge up to a castle and lynch the evil scientist. Danny hadn't expected this much spunk given who they served.

He looked back at the girls. "So, which of you came from this village? It might be best if you led us in."

A group separated themselves and joined Danny at the front. They looked so nervous he felt bad about making them go first. "Don't worry. I'll be right beside you and I won't let any of them hurt you. Come on."

His little speech stiffened their spines, and they led the way down to the village. Once they got close, one of the villagers stepped away from his group, and asked, "Who are you and what business do you have here?"

"My name is Ronin," Danny said. "I'm an adventurer, and I rescued these young ladies from the tower of the one you call the Master of Drakes. I brought them home."

The villager—Danny assumed he served as the mayor or the local equivalent—stared at him with goggled eyes, his pitchfork hanging loose from his hand. "They were supposed to have been sacrificed to the great ones."

Danny shook his head. "Yeah, that was all bullshit. He actually wanted them, or their life force anyway, to power a magic spell. He's been gathering sacrifices for that purpose since your village was founded. It was a good thing I stopped him when I did, because he was getting pretty close to completing it. And if he'd succeeded, none of us would be very happy."

"You opposed the Master and survived?" the mayor asked, seeming in complete disbelief. The rest of the villagers were muttering among themselves as well as looking a good deal less interested in a fight.

"Momma!" one of the girls said.

She sprinted off toward an older woman approaching the gathering from deeper in the village before Danny had a chance to say anything. Their warm embrace did wonders to ease Danny's fears about the sort of greeting the girls would get. Soon the other villagers cast aside their weapons and the former sacrifices mingled with them with much hugging and crying. Everyone else kept their distance, not wanting to intrude on the reunion.

"Did you think it would go this well?" Marlina asked.

"Not hardly." Danny watched the whole thing with a jaundiced eye. It was nice that they welcomed their daughters back, but if they'd been his sisters, no one would've taken them while he still drew breath. That they'd given them up so easily, circumstances be damned, left a bad taste in his mouth.

Finally the reunion broke up and the mayor came closer to Danny. "Will you stay with us for the night? We have only simple food, but there's enough for everyone. I would appreciate it if you'd tell me more about what's going on."

"Sounds good to me. We're totally out of supplies so a meal would be welcome."

Danny fell in beside the mayor with Marlina a step behind. As they walked the mayor said, "The Master was here only a week ago. He emerged from his workshop, spoke with me briefly, then hurried into the forest. We didn't even realize he'd arrived."

The workshop he mentioned had to be a bolt hole. Danny figured he had one. "Can I take a look at his workshop? Also, would you mind going over your meeting in detail?"

"I don't mind, but there isn't much to tell," he said. "We were all startled when a huge red drake flew by. The noise must've drawn the Master's attention and he came out to ask us what happened. I'd barely finished explaining when he turned and ran into the forest. As for the workshop, the Master forbade anyone from entering, but if you're willing to risk it, feel free to look around."

Danny had a really bad feeling about the Master's destination, but he'd have to keep until later. "Thanks. The drake you saw was the queen of the forest. The lady beside me is Marlina, and she's that drake in human form."

The man's eyes nearly fell out of his head. "I didn't know drakes could take on human form. Do you serve the Master?"

"I serve no one," Marlina said, her voice cold. "And only the most powerful greater drakes can shapeshift. I doubt there are more than a handful of us in the world."

"I see," the mayor said. "That's reassuring and I meant no offense. We were taught that all the drakes in the forest served the Master and that was how he kept us safe. It seems many of the things our ancestors taught us were false."

"It's not your fault you were lied to," Danny said. "But what you decide to do next will be your responsibility. The Master… Does this guy have a name? Calling him by his self-proclaimed title is getting on my nerves."

"We've never called him anything but Master," the mayor said.

"We never exchanged names," Marlina added.

"Whatever. Anyway, he's not going to be here to control you anymore, or to protect you. The five villages are going to have to make some important decisions about their future."

"Five villages?" the mayor said. "I thought we were the

only one. It seems a great deal has been going on in the forest that I knew nothing about."

The mayor stopped in front of a hut that looked no different than any of the others and said, "Let's continue this discussion in my home. The others will help your companions settle in and feed them. My name is Timothy, by the way."

"Pleasure," Danny said. "Hopefully we can sort things out tonight. If I'm right about his destination, I want to give your former master as little time in the castle as possible."

CHAPTER 22

Danny belted on his sword and headed for the door. He'd spent the night sleeping on Timothy's living room floor. Not the most comfortable of beds, but he'd been too exhausted to complain. He wanted to get going this morning before everyone else woke up. Good-byes were not his favorite thing.

Not to mention that if all went well he hoped to be back in a week at most. Timothy offered him enough supplies to last that long as well as promising to contact the other villages and bring them up to date on the current situation. Danny appreciated not having to handle that conversation. Getting your entire worldview turned on its head wouldn't be an easy thing to accept.

With matters here as settled as he could make them, he needed to head for the castle and finish things. He'd be shocked if he didn't find the Master of Drakes waiting for him. Leastways he hoped the elf-blood would be. Until he killed the son of a bitch Danny wouldn't feel confident about the girls', not to mention the entire region's, safety.

He tightened his last bootlace and headed for the door. Outside, a beautiful summer morning greeted him. The weather felt far too nice to waste the day hunting a psycho wizard. A picnic and fishing would suit him much better. Maybe one day he'd actually have a chance to do that, but for now he had ether pools to destroy.

He sensed Liana approaching from deeper in the village and a moment later she came into view as she strode up the road. She slept in a different hut last night and he'd assumed that, as busy as they'd been lately, she'd sleep in. Looked like he was mistaken.

Danny paused to let her catch up. She still wore his spare tunic though someone had loaned her a proper pair of shoes, albeit ones at least a size too big. It should've been comical, but she made it look hot.

"Morning," he said. "Figured you'd still be asleep."

"I had a feeling last night you'd be leaving early. I didn't want to miss out on saying goodbye."

"That was thoughtful, thanks."

"You're going to fight him again."

It wasn't a question but he nodded anyway. "Yup. He got away last time, but this time he won't be so lucky. Once he's dead, everyone, including the drakes, will be safe. At least as safe as anyone can be in this world."

"Be careful." She closed the distance between them and wrapped her arms around him.

Liana's trembling surprised him less than the hug. As he feared, she'd gotten attached during their time together.

"I will be. Don't worry, I'll be back in a few days, a week at most. Then we'll see about figuring something out for the villages."

"And once you do that?"

He sighed. "Then I move on. The ether pools won't destroy themselves, more's the pity. Don't worry, you'll be fine. You're tougher than you give yourself credit for."

She stepped back, hesitated, then surged closer, stretching up on her tiptoes and kissing him full on the lips. When she pulled back this time she said, "Something for you to think about. Maybe hanging around here wouldn't be so bad."

He had no chance to say anything else before she spun and hurried back the way she'd come.

Well, as goodbyes went, that one was pretty nice. It wouldn't change his plans, but it would make a pleasant memory. Danny headed down the road toward the nearby forest. A dark figure waited for him right at the edge of the trees.

Marlina offered a warm smile as he approached. "I was going to offer to come with you, but I don't imagine you'll need any help."

"I wouldn't turn you down, but I also wouldn't ask you to return to your prison. I'm sure there are plenty of bad memories at the castle."

"You're far too thoughtful for a human. I expect you to return safely."

"I'll do my best. One thing you could do is make sure the other drakes keep well clear of the castle. When I destroy the ether pool, the energy released is liable to obliterate everything within a half mile or so. I'd feel bad if anything happened to them."

"I'll spread the word. I'll also hang around here to make sure no one bothers the villagers."

"I appreciate it. See you later." With a final smile, he

walked past her and broke into a run. Hopefully this would be his last run through the forest for a while.

Calum didn't know how long he'd been floating in the vat, surrounded by crimson liquid and wracked with pain, but when the fluid began to drain out, taking the pain with it, he'd never felt more relieved. The process took most of a minute then an invisible energy field dried him as his lungs heaved and he coughed up mouthfuls of the horrid, bitter fluid. When he finished coughing, the cylinder split in the middle and he staggered out.

His head spun and his muscles trembled as he struggled to stay upright. He raised a shaking hand to wipe his face and froze. Glistening red scales covered the back of his right hand. Curved black talons tipped each finger. Heart racing as panic spread through him, he shoved up his sleeve. More red scales ran all the way up his arm.

He'd gotten his hand back, but at what price?

"You look less than pleased." Tharion's spirit wavered into view.

"What have you done to me?" Calum demanded.

"I've improved you," Tharion said. "Now you're at least a marginally acceptable replacement guardian for the ether pool. You should be honored."

"Honored?" Rage ignited in Calum, burning away the shock. He took a step toward the spirit as if he could thrash its incorporeal body. "I'm an elf-blood, a descendant of Heaven! I needed no improvements!"

Tharion scoffed. "Please, spare me your outrage. You

carry the barest trace of the blood of Heaven. You're hardly better than an unusually long-lived human. Now, at least, you might prove useful as a guardian."

"I am not your servant. I have my own plans and they don't involve being your guard dog!" Calum snarled and gathered ether. Or at least he tried to. As soon as he attempted to form a spell, his mind went blank and the magic fizzled. If his appearance surprised him, being unable to cast left him stunned.

Tharion chuckled. "You're bound to the castle now. You can only use your magic outside its walls. You should—"

He fell silent, head cocked as if hearing something Calum couldn't. "An intruder is approaching the castle. I would've liked to give you more time to acclimate to your new body, but it seems you'll have to learn the hard way. Make no mistake, you belong to me, Calum Thorne. Accept your fate and dispatch the intruder. Now."

The spirit pointed at a glowing square on the floor near the chute that delivered Calum to this cursed fate in the first place.

Calum wanted to howl his rage and frustration, but his body was already moving of its own accord. As soon as he reached the glowing square, it rose, carrying him up to the library. He emerged from another opening in the floor and stepped off. The opening vanished as soon as he got clear.

He walked, puppet-like, out of the library. Step by step despair replaced anger. Was this to be his fate? Enslaved for eternity, a helpless thrall to a spirit's whims? All his years of effort, only to end up reduced to this miserable state was beyond pathetic.

He reached the massive double doors and flung them

open. Whatever fool came here uninvited would soon regret it. He planned to vent all his frustrations on them.

A lone figure strode straight toward him, a bladeless hilt gripped in his hand.

Ronin.

Heaven hadn't abandoned him fully. Though a slave, at least he'd have his revenge.

Danny left the forest and entered the clearing around the castle. He'd rested for a full twelve hours before closing in. He wanted to be at his best for the fight he knew was coming. Despite the bright sunlight, the looming castle looked especially dark. Probably his imagination, but the sight gave him the creeps all the same.

He pulled the ethersword out of storage, but didn't light it. At the first sign of trouble that would change, but for now he'd bide his time.

Halfway to the main gate, the huge double doors swung open. Beyond them stood the Master of Drakes. At least Danny was pretty sure it was him. He had on the same outfit, but his right hand had grown back, sort of. It looked like a drake's foot, with long black nails and red scales visible on his wrist. More scales had grown across his forehead and under his eyes as well as on his left hand. No doubt more covered the rest of his body.

How the hell had such a transformation happened? It hadn't been *that* long since their first battle. Certainly it didn't seem like enough time had passed for such a remarkable change.

"What happened to you?" Danny asked.

"There was a price for getting a new hand. A hand you took from me. I intend to pay you back and then some for all the trouble you've caused."

Danny met the Master's glare with one of his own. "You used the life force of innocent girls in some weird magical ritual and made slaves of the drakes. You got what you had coming."

A growl rumbled deep in the Master's throat. No normal man had ever made a sound like that. "I will not be lectured by the likes of you!"

He stepped out of the castle and threw a hand forward. Fire roared out in a blazing torrent.

Danny dove aside but the flames scorched him in passing. Ignoring the smell of singed hair, he rolled to his feet and lit the ethersword.

Another stream of flames forced him away from the castle. Danny dodged blast after blast. He was in no great danger of getting hit, but he couldn't close the gap either.

He sent ether through the mithril hilt and used the enhanced energy to hurl a bolt of lightning.

The Master spun away, avoiding the blast. The door behind him was less fortunate. Danny's spell blew a jagged hole in it.

More fire streams drove Danny further back. The Master followed for a few strides before stopping.

Danny frowned as he ducked under a weak blast. A shield appeared in front of him and the flames splashed against it without doing any harm. At this range the flames had no hope of breaking through Danny's defenses, yet the Master didn't come any closer.

The moment he figured it out, Danny wanted to slap his

forehead. The Master stood the same distance from the castle as Marlina used to. Someone had bound him to the castle. Whoever transformed him into…whatever the hell he was now, had also made him the new guardian of the ether pool.

Danny grinned. He could win this fight without closing in. Every infantryman loved artillery support. A few full-power, mithril enhanced blasts should do the trick. If he happened to level the castle in the process, well, digging through the rubble to reach the ether pool shouldn't take that long.

Ignoring the weak splashes of fire flaring against his shield, Danny gathered power, compressing it into the shape of an artillery shell. As Lyra had taught him, having a clear image made the magic easier and Danny knew these shells like the back of his hand.

When the spell started to grow unstable, he hurled it at the Master.

He tried to raise a barrier. Danny gave him credit for that. Then the shell exploded and a mini mushroom cloud rushed into the air. The roar of the blast, even muted by Danny's protective magic, nearly deafened him.

When the smoke cleared, the Master and the castle still stood, though a section of stone had been blown off the wall revealing the smooth steel underneath. Interesting, he'd been wondering why the elves built a stone castle, but it seemed the stone served a purely decorative function.

"Coward!" the Master shouted. "Fight me face to face!"

Danny just rolled his eyes. Don't hide and attack from ambush. Don't use artillery. Did this idiot know nothing about how battles were fought?

Whatever. Now that he'd seen the results, he was sure a

couple more shots would finish the job. He began building another shell, focusing this time on increasing the pure concussive force and eliminating the fire. Clearly the Master's new body resisted heat and flames, so no sense wasting any power on that.

When the spell began to tremble, Danny hurled it and quickly added a sound barrier to his shield. The shell exploded a moment later. More chunks of stone went flying. The force of the blast sent the Master hurtling backwards to slam into the castle wall with hopefully bone-breaking force.

Danny watched for a few seconds, but the mutated figure stayed still. A few hints of his life force remained so the spell hadn't killed him outright. Maybe the blast knocked him out.

Whatever the case, he didn't look capable of continuing the fight. The two blasts had taken a fair chunk of Danny's strength. Seeing no reason to waste any more power, he strode toward the castle, intent on finishing things up close and personal.

Danny picked his way around the few chunks of stone that had fallen from the wall, every sense alert for signs of spellcasting. He needn't have worried. The Master didn't so much as flinch when Danny closed the distance between them.

Still wary of some final treachery, Danny kept the ether-sword lit and between himself and the Master. The final blast had reduced his green robe to tatters. The red scales on his back were cracked and shattered. Blood oozed from numerous wounds.

Danny toed him over. Hate-filled eyes glared up at Danny. "You couldn't even give me the dignity of death in a fair fight? I suppose expecting honor from a human was unreasonable."

"What does honor have to do with fighting? You tried to kill me and I tried to kill you back. My strategy was better than yours which is why I'm standing and you're lying there bleeding. Had you been something other than a psychopath who hurt innocent people, we might've gotten along."

The Master made a noise that was somewhere between a cough and a laugh. "Me, be friends with a human? I'd see myself in hell first."

"Okay." Danny swung the ethersword, separating the Master's head from his neck. He waited a couple seconds just to make sure, but it looked like that finished things. Danny shook his head at the waste of life. The Master of Drakes could've done a lot of good in the world had he chosen a better path.

Oh well. Life was full of disappointments. Time to get on with his real mission.

Danny stepped over the headless corpse and entered the castle. The interior echoed other elf-blood structures he'd visited. Extremely light on decorations, lots of plain steel, and damn little personality.

He went room by room, ethersword at the ready and defensive spells in place. Someone must have caused the Master's weird transformation: the ether pool's true guardian, Danny assumed. He, she, or it had to be around here somewhere and he was pretty sure the guardian wouldn't let Danny complete his mission without a fight.

It took most of an hour to search the first floor and Danny came up empty. He found nothing of interest beyond some old furniture and no way down to the pool. He debated just cutting a hole in the floor but decided to save that as a last resort.

Instead he made his way up the staircase to the second

floor. The first few rooms looked pretty much the same as the ones on the first floor, then Danny found the library.

It didn't hold a candle to the one in Elfhome, but he figured there had to be a few hundred books on the shelves. Good thing he found this place before destroying the ether pool. It would be a shame to destroy so much knowledge.

Danny got busy loading the books into his storage. Nothing bothered him as he worked and he was starting to think he guessed wrong about a second guardian. Not that he planned to complain. He wasn't exactly a huge fan of battles to the death.

Danny emerged from his storage after dropping off the last load of books and dusted his hands off. Okay, that was that. Now to find a way to the pool. Streams of ether ran down to it, but the walls and floors proved no barrier to magical energy. Danny was less fortunate.

Out of the corner of his eye he spotted a statue of a severe-looking elf-blood man. How had he missed that earlier? Too focused on the books probably. A plaque at the statue's feet had something written on it.

Curious, Danny went over for a closer look. When he was about to crouch, a trapdoor opened under his feet and the next thing he knew he found himself sliding down a smooth metal chute into the darkness.

CHAPTER 23

The steel slide went on for far longer than Danny expected. All he could see were the smooth sides in the light of his ethersword. He debated trying to slow himself down, but the chute went in the direction he wanted to go, so he settled for enhancing his body and hoping for the best.

Half a minute later he dropped straight down into a glass cylinder. The impact sent vibrations up his legs but did him no harm. He looked up in time to see the opening seal shut. No getting out that way.

Beyond the clear glass a wizard's lab spread out before him. Shelves of alchemical equipment lined the walls. Two rows of tables, some etched with magic circles and others covered with pristine equipment ready for use, filled the bulk of the space. Danny didn't recognize most of the items. Apparently his host body hadn't spent much time studying alchemy. The most important thing was a distinct lack of an ether pool.

Looked like he needed to delve deeper yet.

A ghostly figure materialized before him, hovering just beyond the glass. Its features, despite being see through, were unmistakably those of an elf-blood. The high cheekbones, pointed ears, and arrogant sneer could belong to no other demographic. Danny sensed no aura of corruption at least, so he wasn't dealing with an undead or demon. What he actually was dealing with, on the other hand, Danny had no idea.

"I assume you're the one who freed my first guardian and slew the second." The specter's voice sounded as arrogant as the rest of him looked. "Quite a feat for a mere human."

"Thanks. I suppose that makes you the one who transformed the Master of Drakes into whatever the hell he was at the end."

"Correct. My name is Tharion Dusk and this is my castle. Now I find myself in need of a replacement guardian. You'll do nicely once we make a few modifications."

"That's going to be a no from me." Danny touched the etherblade to the glass and slowly sliced a vertical line through it. Next he added a couple horizontal cuts. A final burst of power sent pieces of glass flying across the lab. Danny stepped down and brushed a few stray shards off his tunic.

Tharion stared at Danny, his translucent features flickering with barely restrained fury. "Do you realize that I'll never be able to replace that cylinder? It's not like I have spares in the closet. You are damaging the finest alchemy lab in the world."

Danny shrugged. "It's going to end up vaporized once I destroy the ether pool. But I'll tell you what, if you guide me to the pool, I'll leave everything here alone. Deal?"

"Don't be foolish. Wait, I'm speaking to a human after all,

so that might be too much to ask. In any case, the ether pool is incredibly durable. You'll never be able to destroy it."

"I destroyed the first. Can't see why this one would be so much tougher." Danny concentrated and sent a pulse of ether into the floor. Like sonar, it bounced back and confirmed the presence of a tunnel under the lab.

One of the tables blocked his path so he kicked it aside. Glass vessels shattered and metal utensils clattered across the floor.

"Savage! Must you destroy my possessions so casually?"

"No. At this point I'm just doing it for fun." He drove the ethersword into the steel floor up to the hilt and cut a slow circle. When it was complete, the heavy metal plate crashed down into the tunnel below "There we go."

He saw no sign of the ether pool, but the tunnel did run for quite a ways in both directions. Looked like he had some walking to do.

Danny hopped down, landing with a metal clang on the steel disk. Unlike everything he'd seen so far, the tunnel had been carved out of stone. Visions of autonomous diggers danced in his head for a moment, but now that he knew how to deal with them, the giant constructs frightened him a good deal less.

He checked the ether and found it flowing down and to his right. The tunnel curved around beyond his sight, but he assumed it would eventually lead to his destination.

Danny caught a flicker of movement in his peripheral vision, spun, and slashed. Right through Tharion's ghost or whatever he was.

The elf-blood's arrogant face was twisted up, livid with rage.

"You look upset," Danny said. "I recommend you stay

behind since I'll be happy to slice through anything that gets in my way."

"Why destroy the ether pool?" Tharion asked. "What could you possibly hope to gain from such wanton destruction? Maybe we can make a deal. I still have all the knowledge I possessed in life. Surely a trade isn't beyond the realm of possibility."

"Unless you know another way to sever the link between Earth and Valindor, we've got nothing to discuss."

Danny set out and Tharion floated along beside him. He felt a bit like Scrooge with one of his ghostly guides, only his didn't have any useful life lessons to impart.

The tunnel angled down in a spiral which tightened with every stride. Given how far he'd gone, Danny figured he had to be getting close. Nothing had tried to kill him in a while which he found both strange and welcome. Maybe Tharion and his guardian were the only things protecting this place.

Speaking of his ghostly elf-blood companion, he'd been awfully quiet for the last little while. Probably plotting something, though with his limited means to directly manipulate the world, Danny had no idea what he might manage.

At last the passage opened into a square chamber identical to the one he'd found beneath the crystal mine. The ether pool glowed with the same blue light and matching runes ringed the opening. Danny ignored the pool for the moment, went to the wall, and slashed across it.

"What are you doing now?" Tharion sounded so pained it made Danny smile.

"The last pool had some nasty autonomous diggers hiding in the walls. They didn't activate until I tried to damage the pool. If this one has something similar lying in wait, I'd prefer to deal with them before they wake up."

Slash after slash, he checked all the way around the chamber and found nothing hidden. That pretty much confirmed his theory that all the guardians were upstairs.

Satisfied, Danny strode to the pool's edge, raising his blade.

"Wait, please!" Tharion said. "I admit I know of no way to several the ethereal link, but surely with a few hundred years of research..."

Danny laid the ethersword's blade on the nearest rune. "I don't have hundreds of years. Human, remember?"

The light turned red and the recorded Elvish message, the same one as the first time he did this, rang out. He didn't bother to translate it. Instead he tensed in anticipation of some final attack.

None came and eventually the sword cut through the rune, breaching the pool's containment magic. The warning changed and Danny recognized his cue to split.

He turned for the tunnel and ran. Tharion glided along beside him, flickering in and out of existence. He never said anything. Maybe damaging the pool had left him incapable of speech. A small mercy for Danny.

The winding tunnel blurred past as he pounded up the passage. He sprinted right by the hole he'd cut. There was no easy way out of the lab so he'd take his chances following the tunnel. There had to be an exit at the far end.

Or so he assumed. The tunnel ended in a solid sheet of steel. Well, if there was no door, he'd just have to make one. Danny stabbed the blade into the metal and got to cutting. The elf-blood's steel resisted the same as always. The ether grew more turbulent the closer the pool came to destruction.

He needed to hurry.

"Come on, come on," Danny muttered as he cut the final side.

When the rough door was finished, he sprinted out into the castle's great hall. From there he had a straight shot through the door and into the forest. Tharion had disappeared at some point, but Danny didn't give the ghost more than a passing thought.

Escaping the impending blast took all his attention.

As soon as the thought formed, a horrible roar filled the air and a blinding light washed over him. Danny grimaced against the glare, but at least nothing hurt. Looked like he'd gotten just far enough away.

He slowed and when the light faded turned back. Through the gaps in the trees, he spotted a blackened circle. Looked like he'd cleared the danger zone by only a couple hundred yards.

That was a damn sight closer than he would've preferred, but all was well that ended well. Now to get back to the village. Marlina and Liana would probably be worried about him.

Liana paced at the edge of the village. Every few minutes her gaze shifted to the nearby forest. She couldn't stop thinking about Ronin. He was so strong, but so was the Master of Drakes. If the two fought, she wasn't sure he'd come out of it alive. And she very much wanted him to come back safe. Even if they didn't have a future together, and she was honest enough to admit that the odds of him settling down in her village and raising crops and a family were pretty small, she still wanted him to be okay.

She dragged her gaze away from the trees and turned back to the village. The heads of the other four villages had arrived that morning. She was stunned to learn how close they were yet she had never known they existed. Not that exploring a forest filled with meat-eating drakes was the best idea.

A sigh slipped out. Whatever happened next, she knew her life would change forever. None of their lives would be the same.

She considered returning to listen in on the meeting of village leaders but dismissed the idea. Liana was just a girl and no one would pay any attention to anything she had to say.

A pillar of light shot into the sky, forcing her to look away. It came from the same direction Ronin had gone. She chewed her lip. Was it a good sign or a bad sign? She knew so little about magic it hardly bore mentioning.

"You seem concerned." She nearly jumped out of her skin when Marlina spoke right beside her. "No need to be worried about Ronin. I asked a greater wind drake to keep an eye on the castle from a safe distance. He escaped before the blast and is on his way back."

Liana slumped with relief. He was okay. Thank heaven.

She turned to look at the beautiful woman, assuming that was the right word for a transformed greater drake. "Do you love Ronin?"

Marlina blinked, clearly taken aback by the question. "I am grateful to him for freeing me and I very much respect his desire to help both humans and drakes, but love… No, I don't love him, not the way you mean it. Romantic love isn't an emotion drakes experience."

Now it was Liana's turn to be confused. "Really? I thought everyone felt love."

"It's very likely because drakes don't reproduce the way humans do. We require no mates. In fact, we tend to be solitary creatures, keeping to our own territory. The closest thing we have to human love is the affection we feel for our young and that tends to fade over time. Some lesser drakes abandon their eggs as soon as they lay them."

Liana wasn't sure what to make of all that, but since Marlina seemed chatty, she asked, "What's going to happen to us now?"

"That's up to you. As Ronin requested, I'll tell the drakes not to attack humans. Your villages will be safe from my kind. What you do and how you live is outside my control. Now that you're free, I hope you make good choices."

Liana hoped so too. Though what those choices would look like, she was uncertain.

CHAPTER 24

A few days of walking brought Danny back to the edge of the village where he left the girls. It had been more like a stroll than the forced rush of his trip to the castle. With the Master of Drakes dead and the ether pool destroyed, Danny had pretty much finished his work in this part of the world. Once he cleaned up a few loose ends, it would be time to set out for the next target. He had plenty of time to reach the Ice Fang Mountains before it got too cold. He'd find the next closest ether pool there.

But first things first, he wanted to help set up the villagers. Assuming they were interested, his plan would benefit them and the Wizards' Guild.

At the edge of the village he found Marlina waiting. Danny smiled as he approached. "This is a nice greeting. Anything exciting happen while I was gone?"

"Not really. The leaders of the other villages arrived and they've been having some serious conversations. I saw the pillar of light. I take it the ether pool is no more."

"Yup. The Master of Drakes is dead as well. The weird thing was, I ran into a ghost or something named Tharion Dusk. He said the castle was his."

Marlina's smile vanished. "He was the half-elf who made the flute and bound me to guard the castle. What you met wasn't a ghost but a simulacrum, an artificial copy of his memories and personality. That thing was pretty much all I had for company for centuries."

"Then you have my sympathies. The hour or so I spent with him was enough to last me a lifetime. I wonder if all the half-elves were equally obnoxious."

"I'm pleased to say that I have no idea. Tharion was the only one I had the dubious distinction of meeting."

Danny snapped his fingers. "I had one more question. Do drakes have a favorite sort of meat?"

"Drakes are individuals," Marlina said. "As such they have different likes and dislikes. Why?"

"I was thinking, an easy way for the adventurers to make money and to start not thinking of the drakes as enemies would be for them to offer a goat or sheep or something in exchange for a few scales. The drake could rub against a tree, scrape off any loose scales, and get a free meal out of it. What do you think?"

"I think you might be the only human in the world who would consider trading with drakes rather than hunting and trying to kill them. I'm hesitant to encourage your plan since I'm sure there are humans who would think nothing of using a poisoned animal. A goat dosed with Drake's Bane would be plenty to kill a lesser drake. I think it would be best for our kinds to stay separate."

"I never would've guessed there was a poison especially

effective against drakes. Must be rare." Danny sighed and turned toward the village with Marlina at his side. "I'd like to argue with you, but I've met plenty of the sort of people you're talking about. I'll keep quiet about that plan for now."

"On another subject," Marlina said. "Are you aware that Liana is in love with you?"

Danny shook his head. "She doesn't really know me. She's in love with the idea of the adventurer who saved her life. I can't stay here in any case and I certainly can't take her on the road with me. Before I left, I tried to make that clear to her, but it sounds like I was less effective than I'd hoped. Once I'm gone, she'll get over it and find a nice local boy."

Danny thought he sounded pretty confident, but in truth he had no idea what the future held, for Liana or himself as far as that went. He could only do his best. And right now his best involved talking to the village heads and seeing if they were interested in growing herbs for the Wizards' Guild.

A day of conversations and rest had fully restored Danny's strength. The village heads had been hesitant about his plan to trade with the Wizards' Guild, but in the end they agreed to give it a shot. After all, if it didn't work out they could always stop.

And so he and Liana had set out for Scale City to see what the guild master thought about his plan. Since no one else had ever left the villages, she'd volunteered to serve as a guide for the guild's representative. Though she hadn't said anything, he was pretty sure she also wanted an excuse to spend some more time with him.

The walk through the forest might've taken weeks, but

Danny carried her most of the way and they got within sight of the city walls in just one. He set her down a mile outside the city and they continued on at her pace.

"The trip back is going to take forever," Liana said.

"The guild's representative will probably hire a group of adventurers to guard you, so it'll be safe enough now that the drakes have been told not to attack humans."

She frowned. "Are you not going to lead us back?"

Danny shook his head. He knew this conversation was coming, but they'd been studiously avoiding it. "The whole reason you came with me is to serve as a guide. I hope to be on my way northeast the day after tomorrow at the latest. It's a long run to the mountains and I want to reach them by late summer at worst. You'll be fine."

"I'm not so sure I will. I'll miss you terribly." She clung to his arm as they walked.

He swallowed a sigh. Danny sucked at this sort of thing. Since there was really nothing he could say at this point, he just walked along with her as the city got closer and closer.

No one stood in line at the gate and a force of twenty guards waited outside, spears at the ready. In the center of the group, Mugg stood with his arms crossed, glaring at the two of them.

Liana shifted to stand behind Danny who asked, "What's all this?"

"She's not welcome here," Mugg said. "We don't need that damn wizard and his pets coming back for her again."

"Relax," Danny said. "The Master of Drakes is dead. No one is coming for Liana and she's not staying for long in any case. We have business at the Wizards' Guild. I expect we'll both be out of your hair in a couple days."

Mugg's eyes narrowed. "The wizard is really dead?"

"As a doornail." Mugg's face twisted up in confusion and Danny realized that particular expression must be unused on this world. "I blasted him, cut his head off, and vaporized his body. He's as dead as dead gets. Now, if you'll move out of the way, we'll conclude our business. The sooner that's done, the sooner I can leave this place and never visit again. Doesn't that sound good?"

"That sounds perfect to me," Mugg said. "The sooner you're out of my city, the happier I'll be. Open the gate!"

The portcullis clanked up and the guards made a path for them. Once they were past and on their way to the guild Liana said, "He doesn't like you very much."

"No, he doesn't. I cost him a bunch of money and he took it personally. If he wasn't such a coward, liar, and cheat, we might've gotten along. As things stand, it'll be up to the people of the city to either get rid of him or live with him. It's none of my business either way. Fighting mad wizards is one thing, but I avoid politics."

They reached the guild without incident and Danny knocked. Liana's hands trembled where she held on to his arm. "Don't worry, the guild master here is much more reasonable than Mugg. A low bar I admit, but he struck me as a decent fellow."

The door opened and Howard peered out at them. "Ronin, welcome back. You know non-members aren't allowed inside."

"She's my guest and we've got a business proposal for the guild master. I'm confident he'll want to hear what we have to say."

Howard looked back and forth between Danny and Liana before shrugging and moving aside. "I guess if you're only going to the meeting room it's fine. Come in."

He led them into the greeting area then back to a room with a round table surrounded by chairs. "Wait here. I'll find Master Feral."

"Thanks," Danny said.

Howard closed the door and Danny pulled a chair out for Liana. When she'd settled in, he dropped into the chair beside her.

"Is this going to work out?" she asked.

"I don't see why it wouldn't. Your villages will be growing things they want to buy. Assuming you can agree on a price, the guild should be eager to do business. And if they say no, you're no worse off. We can try working with the adventurers. Don't worry, one way or the other you'll be fine."

She rested her head on his shoulder. "Having you here is very reassuring."

Danny kept quiet. He didn't want to say something that might get her hopes up only to dash them again.

Thankfully the door opened before the quiet grew awkward and Feral strode in. He looked them over then his gaze settled on Danny. "I didn't expect to see you again so soon, and with a charming companion no less. Howard mentioned a business proposal. We're still light on capital after buying the drake carcass, so I'm not sure how much we'll be able to offer."

"This isn't an immediate-coin thing but a possibly ongoing arrangement. Pull up a chair and we'll tell you about it."

Feral did so and Danny gave him a highly edited version of the past few weeks. When he got to the end of the story he said, "I offered to act as a go-between for the villagers, but you'll have to discuss the purchase of herbs with the headmen yourself. Liana here can guide you to them. The drakes won't attack humans as long as you leave them alone, but you still might want to hire some guards to chase away any wild beasts you might encounter."

Feral stayed quiet for a few seconds, his face a blank mask. Danny couldn't begin to guess if the suggestion pleased him, pissed him off, or something else. At last the guild master said, "That's a remarkable story. It's a relief to know the wizard has been dealt with permanently. The threat of someone showing up with a force of drakes is not a pleasant one. And a steady source of herbs would be most welcome. Do you think they'd be willing to listen to our requests in regard to which varieties to grow?"

Danny glanced at Liana who started then said, "I'm sure they would. This is all new for us, so your help would be most welcome."

"You might be able to work with them to collect samples," Danny said. "That way you can be sure to get exactly what you want."

Feral nodded. "That's a splendid idea. Howard's been eager for more responsibility, this'll be a good project for him. One question if I may."

Danny nodded.

"Why are you coming to us rather than the Adventurers' Guild?"

"Are you serious? I don't want Mugg anywhere near these people. I don't trust the man as far as I could throw him. He's also a cheat and I'd be delighted if he didn't see a single copper coin from this project, though if you hire adventurers, I suppose it's impossible to avoid him completely. Do you disagree with my assessment?"

"Sadly no. Mugg is too embedded in the city to remove easily, but I think for the general good of Scale, it may be necessary at some point. But that's a problem for down the road. When can you be ready to leave?"

Danny looked to Liana.

"Um, in the morning, I guess," she said. "It's too late now."

"That's fine," Feral said. "I'll speak to Howard and see about guards. I'll keep the post as vague as possible. What say we meet here an hour after sunrise?"

"That's fine," Liana said. "Thank you."

"No, thank you, young lady," Feral said. "Having reliable suppliers rather than depending on the odd delivery of herbs will make our business more reliable. That should lead to greater profits for all of us."

Danny stood and held out his hand. The two men shook and he said, "I'll swing back by this way when my other work allows. You know, just to make sure everything is going smoothly."

Feral's grimace indicated he understood very well what Danny was saying. Should he try to screw over the villagers, there would be a reckoning.

Liana shook hands with him as well and Danny led her outside. Once they were a block away from the guild she asked, "What now?"

"We'll find an inn nearby and get you settled. Then I need to buy supplies. It's a pretty long ways to the Ice Fang Mountains."

"Can I come with you?"

"Sure, if you want to. I'm just going to buy all the food I can find as well as ropes and other mountain gear. Shouldn't take long."

She latched on to his arm and they set out for the merchants' area. Danny enjoyed the sausages he got last time and hoped they'd have plenty in stock. Though in this world, you really couldn't count on finding the same thing two visits in a row.

Beside him, Liana looked happy just to tag along. Danny hoped she found someone nice and lived a happy life. Given all she'd been through, she deserved it.

BONUS CHAPTER 1 - HEAVENLY DEBATE

In a glowing, quiet section of Heaven that Adonael considered hers, at least as much as any section of Heaven belonged to anyone, the archangel worked to transform a group of newly arrived souls into elves. They were all that remained of some of her finest knights on Valindor. She had commanded them to slay the hero, Daniel, for his stubborn refusal to obey her commands and abandon the quest to destroy the summoning circle that connected Valindor to his Earth.

The knights had failed, miserably, in their task. Which didn't surprise her. As the hero, even diminished by his resurrection, Daniel was without a doubt a force to be reckoned with. But even he would be no match for a full squad of elves. Summoning them would be a trying task for her priests, but if enough of them gathered together, they could do it. Figuring out the best possible circumstances to trap and kill the human would be tricky, but far from impossible.

"Adonael." She winced when the Goddess spoke to her. "Are you planning to send those elves against Daniel?"

It was a rhetorical question since the very nature of Heaven made it impossible for them to keep secrets from each other. Nevertheless she answered. "You know I am. He must be stopped before the link is severed. Two pools have already been destroyed, something I wouldn't have thought possible. If I don't act quickly, who knows how much trouble he might cause."

"Or how much good he might do. Daniel has already helped stop the spread of a plague, freed a greater drake from slavery, and rescued many innocent people. He is a hero in the truest sense of the word. The elves' purpose is to defeat evil. You can't send them against someone who has done so much good."

"I'm the primary overseer of Valindor," Adonael said. "It's my decision."

"Daniel isn't native to Valindor. He comes from an Earth where I am the primary overseer. That puts him under my jurisdiction."

"I don't believe that's correct. The elves are going as soon as I can arrange to have them summoned."

"I'm calling a conclave. You're misusing Heavenly resources."

If she'd had a physical form, Adonael's jaw would've dropped. There hadn't been a proper conclave since just before the Binder's fall from Heaven. Surely the Goddess didn't imagine she was in danger of such a fate. Adonael was doing what she had to in order to serve the greater good.

Then why did the prospect worry her so? If she was right, then the others would agree with her.

"Lying to yourself is not an attractive look," the Goddess said.

"So be it. I will abide by the majority's decision. Let the fate of Valindor be on all our heads."

The conclave happened in an instant. As soon as the Goddess's call reached them, the other archangels sent one of their aspects to join the group. There wasn't a discussion since they could all share their thoughts.

To make a formal decision the Goddess asked, "How does the conclave speak? Do we send elves to kill a good man who refuses to follow the will of Heaven or do we let him continue to exercise his freewill?"

"Leave the human in peace," Branik said. "His efforts have served Valindor well."

"You agreed to the summoning and now you'll allow him to destroy all that we've accomplished when we're so close to final victory?" Adonael asked.

"Had you done anything to protect the heroes from their ultimate betrayal, I might have agreed with you. But who can blame Daniel for his decision after what happened to him and those who went before him?"

"That was the choice the mortals made. It wasn't my place to interfere," Adonael said.

"Listen to yourself," the Goddess said. "Does your hypocrisy not disgust you? Murdering the heroes is fine since the human kings made the decision themselves, but when Daniel chooses a path you disapprove of, you want to send elves to kill him."

Adonael's anger and frustration echoed through Heaven. "We're so close to winning this game and five thousand years of peace for Valindor. Don't throw that away for one human. Think of the greater good."

This last plea went to the Binder, but she felt his disapproval. "The hero lived up to his side of the deal, a deal he didn't enter into willingly, and you still let him be killed. There is no honor in that. Let him live his new life as he chooses. Should he fall to evil, then we can send the elves."

Adonael knew she'd lost and a tiny sliver of hate lodged in her essence. How could the others be so foolish?

When the final declarations were made, all opposed her sending the elves to kill Daniel.

The conclave broke up and soon only the Goddess remained. "This is the right thing, you must know that."

"All I know is that you're going to let centuries of hard work and sacrifices be thrown away so one human too arrogant to follow my commands can do as he pleases. For beings dedicated to the greater good, that is beyond madness."

"We all serve the greater good in our own way." The Goddess slowly faded way. "Have a little faith."

Faith? Of all the simpleminded stupidity. The universe continued to exist because Heaven made hard choices. Adonael sometimes had trouble believing such a soft weakling could also be an archangel.

Well, maybe she couldn't send elves, but she wouldn't give up. There had to be a way to preserve the summoning spell. One way or another, she'd find it.

BONUS CHAPTER 2 - THE FIVE KINGDOMS RECOVERY PLAN PART 3

Eve rode south through Villipan surrounded by a squad of ten knights, not ones who answered to Alban Morel, but a group of temple knights dedicated to Branik. True to Adonael's command, Eve had been doing her best to convince King Florian that he needed to work with the other kingdoms to rebuild the army. She wasn't sure if she'd succeeded or if he just wanted her out of his hair, but a week ago Florian had ordered her to act as his emissary to the other kingdoms.

Of all the possibilities Eve had expected, being sent herself hadn't been one of them. She had little experience with diplomacy. Her temple training covered magic and religion. Becoming a diplomat lay well outside her area of expertise. But, if Florian refused to do the right thing, she would make her best effort in his place. At least she'd find out what was happening in the other countries.

She planned to stop in Montreve first. It lay directly to the south of Villipan and had seen little in the way of action during the war. At least as far as she knew. If messages had come from any of the other kingdoms, no one had told her about them. At a minimum, Montreve City, the nation's capital, was the closest after Forte's so it seemed like a good place to start her mission.

She turned a fraction to look at the knight beside her. The young man wore a breastplate over mail along with an open-faced helm. "How far to the border, do you think?"

He jumped when she spoke then said, "I'm not sure, ma'am. The border isn't especially well marked. There are a few forts scattered around, but the soldiers stationed there were largely redeployed north before the war. We could very well be in Montreve already. I believe the commander planned to reach the capital late next week."

Eve smiled. "Thank you. I've never been very good at navigation. Lady Shael always handled that sort of thing when we were traveling with the hero."

"It must've been exciting traveling with those two as well as the other companions."

She nodded. Exciting was one word for her experiences with Lyra and Daniel. Terrifying would be another, and probably the more accurate of the two. "There was certainly a lot more fighting. I'm pleased our trip so far has been peaceful."

A wistful feeling washed over her. Daniel would've told her not to say things like that lest she tempt fate. And maybe he was right. Eve sensed corruption in the distance, perhaps a mile to their west.

"Commander," she said. "I sense demons."

The leader of her guards, a middle-aged knight named Sir Giles, who was also a skilled priest of Branik, shifted in his saddle to look back at her. "How far away?"

"About a mile to our west."

"Hmm. That's on our way to the capital. Can you tell how many there are?"

Eve shook her head. "We're still too far away. As soon as I have a better sense of them, I'll let you know."

"Swords out! Activate divine auras!" Giles said before following his own orders. The knights soon all glowed in the ether as Branik's power surrounded them and enchanted their blades. The magic was similar to what arcane knights did but relied on divine energy.

They rode on, everyone on full alert. The knights' professionalism did wonders to settle Eve's nerves.

Five minutes later Eve said, "I can sense five weak demons and I think four humans. We have to help them."

"So we shall." Giles pointed his sword. "Forward!"

They picked up the pace and soon the site of the battle came into view. Four human warriors battled five of Ardent Lilly's lamprey-headed demons. Six bodies lay unmoving on the ground while twice that many puddles of black sludge marked the end of some demons.

One of the warriors threw a dagger which exploded on impact, sending a demon reeling. She recognized Aline, one of Daniel's companions. Talk about great luck. Surely she could tell Eve what was happening in the kingdom.

Eve didn't need to urge the knights to rescue the survivors. They spurred their horses into the fray, laying about with their enchanted swords until they'd slain all the demons. The battle took only seconds.

She hurried to join them. "Does anyone need healing?"

"Eve?" Aline stared at her. "You're the last person I expected to meet here. What are you doing in Montreve?"

"We're on our way to the capital to speak with the king.

Our goal is to make plans to rebuild the combined army before the demon king returns."

"Daniel killed the demon king," she said.

Before Eve could explain all that had happened since the companions parted ways, Giles said, "Perhaps it would be best if we made camp somewhere away from this mess."

"Good idea," Eve said. "Give me a moment to bless the bodies of the fallen."

Eve climbed down from her horse and approached the nearest corpse. She tried not to look too closely at the horrific wounds that had killed him as she made the halo and bowed her head. Divine energy poured into the body, purifying any lingering corruption and making sure he wouldn't rise again.

When she looked up, Aline stood beside her. She appeared uninjured thank goodness. Though they hadn't been close, Eve was still glad to see the woman unharmed.

"How far is the capital?" Eve asked.

"Ten days or so southwest of here," Aline said. "Don't bother approaching. The city has fallen and is under the thumb of a hellpriest of Ardent Lilly. His Majesty and the royal family made it out alive. For now they're traveling from town to town trying to keep ahead of the demonic forces hunting them. I'm in charge of gathering all the fighters I can and forming a resistance. It's been touch and go."

"I can imagine," Eve said. "Is there somewhere we can make camp around here?"

"There's a walled village maybe five miles away. I've been using it as my base of operations. It's as safe a place as anywhere."

Eve finished blessing the bodies and remounted. Aline

swung up behind her while the other survivors rode double with some of her knights. As they set out Eve said, "We'd hoped to find help, but it looks like you're in no shape to spare fighters for the army."

"You got that right," Aline said. "If the demon king returns, an insane thought if ever I heard one, Montreve wouldn't last a month. How are things in Villipan?"

"We're free of demons and hellpriests, but our fighting forces are reduced to ten percent of what they were before the war. I fear we wouldn't last much longer than Montreve. Do you know how to find the king? I do need to speak with him."

"No, sorry. Since I'm fighting on the front lines, he deemed it unwise for me to know his travel plans. Should I, heaven forbid, end up captured, at least I can't give up their location."

Eve understood the precaution, but it wasn't very handy for her. On the plus side, she did have a vague idea about how she might help both kingdoms and fulfill Adonael's mission. At least she hoped she did.

Brielle was a pretty standard walled town. Eve had visited enough of them over the years and this one had all the usual features. A fifteen-foot-tall palisade with towers manned by archers and a wooden gate that allowed access to the town. Ten guards stood on duty outside and all of them looked exceedingly nervous. Not that she blamed them. Even if they could slip inside and seal the gate in seconds, they were still the most exposed should a force of demons arrive.

In the center of the group stood a priestess of Adonael.

Her white robes had seen better days, but she held herself upright with her shoulders back and her eyes, while shadowed and weary, showed no fear. It was better than Eve could've done had their positions been reversed.

When they got close, Aline hopped off the back of Eve's horse and ran ahead. The conversation was brief and the next thing Eve knew the guards waved them through the gate. As she passed, the priestess bowed. Eve made the sign of the halo and sent a pulse of divine energy into the priestess. Hopefully that would help with her exhaustion. When the magic settled over her, the woman looked up with wide eyes.

Eve smiled. "Keep up the good work, Sister. The Five Kingdoms is counting on all of us."

"I'll do my best, High Priestess." She didn't stammer unlike some of the faithful when they met Eve for the first time.

Inside, it looked like any of a hundred villages in Villipan. The wooden buildings had the same general style. A few businesses were scattered among the homes and warehouses. The handful of people out and about moved with hurried, furtive steps. The constant threat must be wearing on them. Maybe Eve could give a sermon before they moved on to look for the king. She didn't know if it would make any difference, but she'd be glad to try.

Aline led them to the only stone building in the village, a fort built in the center. It wasn't the most impressive thing she'd ever seen, but it did have its own outer wall and a training yard where several dozen fighters were sparring or shooting bows at straw targets.

"You can take your mounts to the stable then we can get a bite to eat in the barracks," Aline said.

Eve turned to Giles. "Could one of you take care of my horse? I want to talk to Aline about something."

"Of course, High Priestess," Giles said. "Leave it to us."

"Thank you." Eve dismounted along with the surviving members of Aline's team.

"Show them to the stable then all of you join us in the barracks," Aline said.

She got a round of salutes then the group was off, leaving the two women alone.

"What did you want to talk about?" Aline asked.

"Villipan. Specifically, King Florian. I'm not sure how much you know about what happened after we parted ways…"

"Damn little." Aline started toward a long, low building near the main keep and Eve fell in beside her. "When we parted company, I joined up with the stragglers from the army and we hurried home. By the time we got here, demons and hellpriests were running around causing chaos. Three weeks after we reached the capital, they forced us to flee. Somehow we got the royal family out in one piece, but it was a near thing. Now we've got groups of resistance fighters doing their best to protect the population centers. The problem is we don't have the numbers to take the fight to the demons."

Inside the barracks' dining hall, Aline led her to an empty table near the back wall. No one else was around at this time of day except the cook and he had plenty do without paying them any attention.

They sat and Eve said, "Things have been pretty bad in Villipan as well and Forte has completely fallen to the demons."

Eve told her about everything save Daniel's resurrection.

"Anyway, King Florian is failing and Adonael is worried we'll have no chance when the demon king returns. I was hoping if we could find King Montreve and bring him to Villipan, he might be able to help bring Florian around or at least minimize the damage Alban is doing."

Aline shook her head. "That's all nuts. I can't believe anyone would be dumb enough to make an enemy of Lady Shael. Outside of the demon king, I can't think of anyone I'd less like to have angry with me."

"You and me both. So, do you think King Montreve will be willing to help?"

"I can't speak for the king, but if we can track him down you can ask. Worst-case scenario he says no. I'll go with you. That way they'll be sure to know you're friendly. The knights were wound pretty tight when I last saw them. They might attack a stranger first and ask questions later."

Eve offered a warm smile of gratitude. "I'd really appreciate it."

"All I'm doing here is getting people killed. Locking down the towns and cities until we can form a proper army is the smarter move."

Eve hated to hear the bitterness in Aline's voice but couldn't deny her words. Hopefully, together, she and King Montreve would be able to set things on a better course. Emphasis on hopefully.

BONUS CHAPTER 3

Carmilla Morain, better known to the world as the demon king, held her hands over the body of the most recent sacrifice and drew the last of his life force into her body. He was strapped to an altar made of ice, his body now reduced to a withered husk. How many lives had she absorbed now, twenty, thirty? She'd lost count, not that it mattered. Every one she killed only increased her power by the tiniest fraction.

When she'd come up with the plan to resurrect herself, Carmilla never imagined it would take this long to recover her former strength. Between dividing her essence into four parts and losing a large portion of each quarter in the ritual, she was barely as strong as your average housewife.

It was pathetic and she hated the feeling. It reminded her of the miserable days before Ardent Lilly spoke to her and granted her the title and power of the demon king. She glanced at the four black-clad attendants waiting silently. They wore the skimpy robes favored by the cult despite the freezing cold of the temple. Magic kept them comfortable while she was reduced to wearing a fur-lined cloak.

She found everything about her current situation intolerable. Only two things comforted her. The first was the knowledge that the cult couldn't kill and replace her. If they did, their master would forfeit the rest of her turn in the great game to claim Valindor. Second, she knew if she was having this much trouble after awakening in the cult's largest temple, her other selves must be struggling even more. The latter was only a good thing in theory since they were all supposed to grow stronger before the final battle to reunite and march once more on the Five Kingdoms.

A dark, familiar presence appeared in the altar chamber. The attendants prostrated themselves while Carmilla took a knee and bowed her head. "Mistress."

"Nahia has failed," Ardent Lilly said. "There will be no easy march for you into the capital."

Carmilla snarled. How could the useless fool have failed so completely? The plan was perfect.

"Like you, the hero survived," Ardent Lilly answered her unspoken question. "And he did so with most of his power intact."

Her jaw dropped. Impossible. How could he still be alive and strong? The only method she could find to bring herself back was the quadripartite resurrection and that had reduced her to this weakened state.

"Heaven's power of creation has ever excelled at this sort of magic," Ardent Lilly said. "Take heart, my Demon King. The hero has lost all desire to fight us. Even now he seeks to sever the connection to Earth seventy-three. You still have time and your path is now clearer than it has ever been. You need only recover your full strength, gather a new army, and complete your mission."

"I've been trying, Mistress, but the process is not proceeding as I would like."

"The master of this temple knows of a powerful source of corruption. It is not of my hell, but it can be converted for your use. Find it, claim it, and complete your task."

Ardent Lilly's presence vanished and Carmilla leapt to her feet. That bastard Xevius had been keeping secrets. How dare the man keep the potential source of ultimate victory from her? Her anger demanded she lash out, but circumstances forced her to stop. She lacked the power to properly punish his duplicity. No, a different tactic would be necessary.

"One of you fetch High Priest Xevius. We have an important matter to discuss."

The attendant nearest the door scurried out. She'd never bothered to learn the girls' names. They were here to amuse her when she was bored and carry out whatever tasks she required. In other words, they were irrelevant.

Fortunately, the high priest must've been nearby as he marched into the altar chamber only minutes after the girl went to fetch him. Xevius was tall, handsome in a dark, violent way, with a perfectly muscled body. His black robe left his chest bare for all to see.

"You summoned me, oh Demon King?" Xevius said.

"Indeed. Ardent Lilly has spoken to me. She says you know about a source of powerful corruption that I might use to speed my recovery. Why is it you haven't shared this information with me?"

Xevius's thin lips turned down and his brow furrowed. A

moment later his eyes widened. "Ah, that place. I truly never imagined it could be of any use to you."

His surprise appeared genuine. That had to mean there were issues that her mistress didn't see fit to mention. Such was always the way when dealing with higher beings. It was so strange the things they felt they could speak about and what they couldn't.

"Perhaps you'd best tell me everything," she said.

"Of course. The power source is a temple of Astaroth that crashed into a mountain not long after you began your first assault on the Five Kingdoms."

"Wait. How does a temple crash into anything? That implies it was in the air at some point."

"That's the scouts' working theory. Some magic must've protected it since it suffered only minimal damage. The temple is seething with corruption. It's also sealed. No one save a priest of Astaroth can open it. So it seems at least. And no one wants that to happen. The Horned One's cult reached it first and their forces aren't letting anyone else close. Astaroth's followers have them surrounded in turn. It's a standoff and none of us has a way to break through both lines. That's why I didn't think to mention it."

Carmilla couldn't fault him for keeping quiet about the temple now that she understood the circumstances surrounding it.

"Can you truly make use of the power?" he asked.

"There is a technique I can use called Dark Syphon. It should be able to transform the corruption enough to make it useful to me. Getting to it will be the bigger problem. None of the other temples are going to let us claim it for ourselves." She snarled her frustration. The potential solution to her problems was right there and she couldn't reach it. "We'll have to keep our eye on the situation and be ready to act when the time is right."

"I have spies watching at all times, rest assured," Xevius said.

"Good. Keep me posted." When the time came, she would seize the power and fulfill her mission. And then the world would belong to Ardent Lilly.

AUTHOR NOTE

Hello everyone,

I hope you enjoyed Danny's latest adventure. Were you surprised to meet Merrok's mom? I'm sure Danny was.

I'll see you next time when we visit the frigid Ice Fang Mountains.

You can sign up for my newsletter at www.jamesewisher.com. and be the first to know when the knew books come out.

As always, thanks for reading.

James E Wisher

ABOUT THE AUTHOR

James E. Wisher is a writer of science fiction and Fantasy novels. He's been writing since high school and reading everything he could get his hands on for as long as he can remember.

ALSO BY JAMES E. WISHER

Summoned to Another Words and Forced to Fight The Demon King

The Summoned Hero

The Birth of Ronin

The Fate of The Five Kingdoms

The Plague Lands

Elfhome

The Forest of Drakes

The Lord of Black Ice

The Immortal Apprentice Trilogy

The War With Audin (Prequel Novella)

The Hunt For Revenge

The Army of Darkness

The Apprentice Reborn

The Soul Bound Saga

An Unwelcome Journey

Darkness in Tiber

Depths of Betrayal

The Black Iron Empire

Overmage

The Divine Key Trilogy

Shadow Magic

For The Greater Good

The Divine Key Awakens

The Portal Wars Saga

The Hidden Tower

The Great Northern War

The Portal Thieves

The Master of Magic

The Chamber of Eternity

The Heart of Alchemy

The Sanguine Scroll

Shadow of The Dragons

The Dragonspire Chronicles

The Black Egg

The Mysterious Coin

The Dragons' Graveyard

The Slave War

The Sunken Tower

The Dragon Empress

The Dragonspire Chronicles Omnibus Vol. 1

The Dragonspire Chronicles Omnibus Vol. 2

The Complete Dragonspire Chronicles Omnibus

Soul Force Saga

Disciples of the Horned One Trilogy:

Darkness Rising

Raging Sea and Trembling Earth

Harvest of Souls

Disciples of the Horned One Omnibus

Chains of the Fallen Arc:

Dreaming in the Dark

On Blackened Wings

Chains of the Fallen Omnibus

The Complete Soul Force Saga Omnibus

The 72 Demons

The Blood of Solomon

A Friend in Need

The Demon Masks

Hunt For The Devil Man

A Family Reunion

The Cursed Fortress

The Aegis of Merlin:

The Impossible Wizard

The Awakening

The Chimera Jar

The Raven's Shadow

Escape From the Dragon Czar

Wrath of the Dragon Czar

The Four Nations Tournament

Death Incarnate

Atlantis Rising

Rise of the Demon Lords

The Pale Princess

Malice

Hearts of Corrupt Fire

Ultima Thule

Aegis of Merlin Omnibus Vol 1.

Aegis of Merlin Omnibus Vol 2.

The Complete Aegis of Merlin Omnibus

Other Fantasy Novels:

The Squire

Death and Honor Omnibus

The Rogue Star Series:

Children of Darkness

Children of the Void

Children of Junk

Rogue Star Omnibus Vol. 1

Children of the Black Ship

Children of The End

www.ingramcontent.com/pod-product-compliance
Lightning Source LLC
LaVergne TN
LVHW090938080826
845145LV00003B/796

* 9 7 8 1 6 8 5 2 0 1 3 1 9 *